Fence Busters

The Chip Hilton Sports Series

For more information on
Chip Hilton-related activities and to correspond
with other Chip fans, check the Internet at
chiphilton.com

Chip Hilton Sports Series
#11

Fence Busters

Coach Clair Bee
Updated by Randall and Cynthia Bee Farley
Foreword by Dean E. Smith

BROADMAN
& HOLMAN
PUBLISHERS

Nashville, Tennessee

© 1999 by Randall K. and Cynthia Bee Farley
Printed in the United States of America

0-8054-1993-4

Published by Broadman & Holman Publishers,
Nashville, Tennessee
Page Design: Anderson Thomas Design, Nashville, Tennessee
Typesetting: PerfecType, Nashville, Tennessee

Subject Heading: BASEBALL—FICTION / YOUTH
Library of Congress Card Catalog Number: 99-26656

Library of Congress Cataloging-in-Publication Data
Bee, Clair.
    Fence Busters / Clair Bee ; updated by Randall and
Cynthia Bee Farley.
        p. cm. — (Chip Hilton sports ; v. 11)
    Summary: As the freshman baseball team at State
University tries to live up to its nickname, "Fence Busters,"
Chip must endure an injury and friction with a jealous
teammate.
    ISBN 0-8054-1993-4
    [1. Baseball Fiction. 2. Sportsmanship Fiction.
3. Universities and colleges Fiction.] I. Farley, Randall K.,
1952– . II. Farley, Cynthia Bee, 1952– . III. Title. IV. Series:
Bee, Clair. Chip Hilton sports series ; v. 11.
PZ7.B38196Fg   1999
[Fic]—dc21   99-26656
                                                        CIP

3 4 5 03 02

TO
LITTLE CYNTHIA ANNE BEE

who so effectively employed a "full nelson" on her father that this book
never made the publisher's deadline

CLAIR BEE
1953

TO

SUZANNE ELIZABETH FARLEY
AND
MICHAEL CLAIR FARLEY

Pop Pop was right when he said,
"Teamwork begins with two or more working as one."

LOVE,
MOM AND DAD
JULY 10, 1999

Contents

CONTENTS

Foreword

WHEN I was ten or eleven years old, I was forced to read books by my parents. Since I liked athletes, I read and enjoyed several books by John R. Tunis that dealt primarily with baseball but also sportsmanship. Now fast forward to the summer of 1959, when at long last I had the opportunity to meet acclaimed basketball coach Clair Bee.

Frank McGuire was a close friend of Coach Bee, and I had just finished my first year as an assistant to Coach McGuire at North Carolina. Coach Bee was helping Frank with his basketball books, *Offensive Basketball* and *Defensive Basketball*. They had asked me to select two topics for chapters in *Defensive Basketball,* so we spent a great deal of time together that summer at the New York Military Academy.

During this period, not only did I stare at the painting of the fictional folk hero—Chip Hilton—that was on the wall behind Coach Bee's dining room table, but I had the opportunity to read some of the Chip Hilton series. The books were extremely interesting and well written, using sports as a vehicle to build character. No one did that better than Clair Bee (although Tunis came close). By that time, Bee's Chip Hilton books had become a classic series for youngsters. While Coach Bee was well known as one of the great coaches of all time due to his strategy and competitiveness, I believe he thought he could help society and young people most by writing this series. In his eyes, it was his "calling" in the years following his college and professional coaching career.

Coach McGuire and I, along with countless other basketball coaches, learned basketball from Clair Bee. The point zone, which Coach Bob Spear and I developed at the Air Force Academy, had its origins in one of Coach Bee's old books on the 1-3-1 rotating zone defense. We made our point zone at Air Force more of a match-up zone, but this is just one instance where people on the basketball court today still depend on innovations by Clair Bee.

From 1959 until his death, I visited with Coach Bee frequently at the New York Military Academy and at Kutsher's Sports Academy, which he directed. He certainly touched my life as a special friend. Not only does he still rank at the top of his profession as a basketball coach, but he now regains the peak as a writer of sports fiction. I am delighted the Chip Hilton sports series has been redone to make it more appropriate for athletics today without losing the deeper meaning of defining character. I encourage everyone to give these books as gifts to other young athletes so that Coach Bee's brilliant method of making sports come to life and building character will continue.

DEAN E. SMITH
Head Coach (Retired), Men's Basketball,
University of North Carolina at Chapel Hill

CHAPTER 1

For the Love of the Game

"THE BASES are loaded! The ducks are on the pond, and varsity coach Del Bennett has called time!"

Gee-Gee Gray, WSUN Radio 1100 sportscaster, flashed a quick smile at Gil Mack, sitting a few feet away in the press box. Mack, sports editor of the *Statesman*, State University's weekly school paper, grinned back at Gray and kept right on tapping the keys of his laptop.

"Three up and three on! Yes, State's freshman phenoms are off to a good start! Coach Bennett's walking slowly out to the mound to visit with Hector 'Hex' Rickard. Bennett's stalling for a little time, hoping to settle down his pitcher and cool off the freshman batters. We're in the top of the first with no one out and no score in this preseason contest between the State University freshman and varsity teams.

"Yes, fans! The freshmen are living up to all of Gil Mack's raves. For the past three weeks he's been touting this team! Gil has tagged them with the nickname 'Fence

Busters.' He just might have something there! They haven't knocked down any fences yet, but two hits and a walk create a lot of possibilities for them. Bennett makes his way back to the dugout."

Directly behind home plate and in the center of a group of State students and longtime baseball fans stood a big man in his forties who was smiling enthusiastically and praising the talents of the Fence Busters. Jim Collins had been hooked on baseball since his earliest memories on the sandlot, and he knew every player on the field.

Jim had been a real ballplayer in his time, a first-rate catcher. The gnarled fingers of his right hand told the story of his old catching days. After those days were over, Collins stuck with the sport: teaching and coaching the game to tee-ballers on up through Little League, following the local high school and university teams, and eating, sleeping, and talking baseball.

Many of his friends worried that Jim Collins had given too much to the sport, woefully neglecting the once large farm that had been in the family for generations and that he had taken over following the death of his father.

Collins was known all over the state. Each year he created files on the top several hundred high school ballplayers around the state who possessed unusual ability and might be interested in coming to State University and learning a lot more about baseball while they earned their degrees. Collins's all-absorbing interest was baseball. And second only to his enthusiasm for the diamond sport was his loyalty to the hometown university.

Jim Collins was a State University booster through and through. He made the rounds of high schools and talked State to every player who wore a pair of spikes, not as an official of the university but as a loyal booster.

FOR THE LOVE OF THE GAME

Cynthia Ann, Jim's only daughter, was a freshman at State. Her father was proud she was realizing the opportunities he had missed. He only wished his wife were still alive to enjoy Cynthia's achievement with him.

In Cynthia's high school years, she and her dad had joked about his dream of having a child who would carry on his baseball prowess and star for State someday. But the dream had never come true. She liked sports and played soccer and softball in high school, but her real interests were writing and books.

Out on the diamond, in the on-deck circle, a rugged freshman tossed two of the three bats he'd been hefting toward the dugout and sauntered slowly up to the first-base side of the plate.

"Who's that, Jim?" someone demanded. "Look at the size of him!"

"Benjamin Cohen," Collins said quickly. "He played tackle on the freshman football team. Great hitter! First baseman. He played for Rockwell at Valley Falls. Hits 'em a mile!"

"Remember 'Mountain' Miller?" another older voice called.

"Looks just like him!"

"His nickname is Biggie," Collins advised. "Six-four and tips the scales at 240."

"Should be Mr. Biggie!" someone snickered. "Looks like he weighs 440!"

"If he doesn't hit better than .440, I'll buy you a season ticket," Collins retorted.

State's varsity was a veteran outfit. League leaders the previous season, the champions had first read Gil Mack's raves about Coach Henry Rockwell's freshman team with tolerant amusement. As the early spring practice weeks slipped away, news of the hitting prowess of the freshmen spread across campus. The varsity stars became sensitive and began anticipating the annual pre-season series to explosively end the myth. The lengthy and glowing articles splashed across the sports pages about the diamond wizardry of State's sensational fresh-man ball club had produced in them a burning resent-ment to show the newcomers who was boss.

Coach Bennett understood the feeling gripping his varsity squad. He knew every player on the field was tense. That was the reason he had called time. And that was the reason he was joking with Hex Rickard and the infielders behind the mound. Bennett talked about everything except the loaded bases. He was stalling for time, trying to relax his veterans. He laughed at his own jokes, slapped Rickard on the back, and walked slowly back to the varsity dugout.

The varsity catcher snickered derisively as he squat-ted behind the plate. "Just another hitter, Hex," he chanted. "C'mon, set him down! He's a looker! No hit! No hit!"

Biggie Cohen never blinked an eyelash; he stood there, his feet spread in a wide stance, with the bat held high and steady.

Hex Rickard reared back and called on all of his tremendous speed to whip the ball down the alley across Cohen's knees.

"S-t-e-e-rike!"

"What'd I tell ya, Hex! C'mon, get him out of here! He's wastin' our time!"

Cohen twisted his spikes a bit more firmly in the clay, pulled his bat through in a practice swing, and waited quietly. Rickard stood behind the mound, polishing the ball and watching the base runners. Speed Morris, dancing off second, kicked up a cloud of dust and yelled something unintelligible to the varsity hurler. Rickard toed the rubber and extended his arms above his head, watching the runner on third intently as he brought the ball down for the pause. Then he dealt what appeared to be another fastball. But it was his famed knuckler.

The ball shot up in the air and then came in fast, twisting and bobbing toward the plate. There was a tense moment of silence and then a sharp crack as Biggie swung too hard, leveling a little under the pitch but still getting a big chunk of the ball. The blow brought a gasp from the crowd as the ball sailed up and up and up, flying high in the air. The ball seemed to hang up there a long time, as though it were looking things over, before it decided to drop lazily behind the right-center wall.

As the ball disappeared, the roar of the crowd crashed out of the stands, and the freshman dugout erupted like a volcano spilling out to greet the grand-slam hitter. Cohen touched all the bases and was mobbed at the plate.

In the grandstand, Jim Collins was pounding someone on the back and yelling, "Didn't I tell you? Didn't I tell you?"

Up in the broadcasting booth, Gee-Gee Gray yelled, "There's a high floater out to right center, and that ball is going . . . going . . . gone! What a smack! And he only got a piece of it!"

Gil Mack waved his two keyboarding hands in the air and yelled, "Fence Busters! Fence Busters! Fence Busters!"

Now the mob of students and fans who had been fired with curiosity began to appreciate all the talk about the competition between the freshman stars and the veteran diamond champions. The big turnout was unusual, to be sure, but this freshman team was unusual too. The fans were still discussing Cohen's base-clearing homer when Ellis "Belter" Burke strolled up to the plate.

Burke changed the conversation by driving Rickard's first pitch straight as a bullet all the way to the right-field fence. That whack smacked the fence, the ball bounding sharply away before the sound had echoed back to the grandstand. Burke pulled up to second.

Andre Durley followed with a hard single over short-stop, and Burke was held at third. The fans were on their feet now, stomping and cheering. Then Murphy "Murph" Gillen, the powerful first-year right fielder, lashed a vicious liner down the third-base line, helping Burke score and sending Durley to third. Gillen pulled up at second. Darrin Nickels, the 230-pound catcher, added to the pandemonium when he cracked the ball over first base. The clothesline drive kicked up the lime and bounded into the corner of right field. Durley and Gillen scored, and Nickels held up at third. The noise of the crowd was one continuous roar as Terrell "Flash" Sparks, the starting pitcher, stepped up to the plate.

"Hey, Rockwell's got Sparks batting. Where's the des-ignated hitter?" a student seated near Collins wondered out loud.

"Looks like Rockwell has decided to see what his pitchers can do at the plate," observed Collins. The grandstand fans listened eagerly now as he reeled off the stats on the husky hurler. "Six feet, 200 pounds, and all muscle!" Collins shouted excitedly. "Every team in the big leagues had scouts camped on his doorstep last May."

"Bet you were there too," someone yelled mockingly.

Collins beamed. "You know it!" he called, nodding his head. "Kids who get a chance to go to college shouldn't pass up the opportunity."

"Especially if they're big-league caliber and have a chance to go to State," the same loud voice interrupted.

The pointed remark brought a flush to Collins's face, but he controlled the angry retort poised on his lips. "That's right," he said grimly, his lips clamped in a tight, straight line. "Especially to State! You know any other institution that's done more for people like you and me?"

There was no reply to that one. State University was an all-encompassing institution in the most complete sense, providing its students with educational, economic, social, and cultural advancement. Most on- and off-campus programs focused on business administration, science and technology, the arts, medicine, law, engineering, and the all-important field of education.

Flash Sparks had broad shoulders and big hands. He handled the long bat as though it were a toothpick. But he was too eager. He swung from his heels on every pitch and went down after three straight. Ozzie Crowell, the freshman leadoff hitter, sauntered up for his second time at bat in the inning. Crowell was a squat, bowlegged, power-packed second baseman, a peppery holler guy. But Hex Rickard was bearing down now, and he sent his southpaw sliders blazing in and down around Crowell's knees for his second-straight strikeout.

Speed Morris, the freshman shortstop sensation, caught Rickard's first pitch on the nose, driving the ball right back up the alley. The ball was a flash of light, but Hex knocked it down and threw Speed out at first by a whisker to retire the side.

The freshmen got a tremendous hand when they charged out on the field, and the big seven on the scoreboard seemed like a lot of runs. But State's upperclassmen were pretty good ballplayers too. And they were hot about the first inning. They pounced on Sparks's offerings with grim determination and got themselves five runs on four hits, two walks, and two errors. The bases were loaded when Biggie Cohen leaped high in the air to pull down a hard smash headed for short right field.

"Good hit, no field, Jim," someone in the grandstand chided.

"The Rock will take care of that," Collins retorted.

"He won't have to teach that big first baseman much!"

There was no doubt the freshmen could hit. The following innings proved that. But their play in the field was a different story. The varsity players couldn't match their opponents' power hitting, but they took full advantage of every miscue and every show of indecision and made the freshmen "throw the ball." Perhaps "heave the ball" was more like it. Anyway, the freshmen's fielding misplays kept the varsity in the ball game.

There wasn't a zero on the scoreboard when the varsity came in for its last swings in the bottom of the ninth. And the score sounded more like that of a football game than baseball. The freshmen were leading 29-28. During the hectic struggle, Henry Rockwell had called on three pitchers. Sparks, yanked in the third, had been followed by Silent Joe Maxim. Lefty Byrnes had relieved Maxim in the eighth. Del Bennett had used four hurlers.

The fans were limp, hoarse, and worn out. Collins was the lone exception. Jim was just as fresh and enthusiastic as he'd been during the first pitch of the game.

"Byrnes will go to work now," Collins said confidently, "now that the chips are down. He'll set 'em down one-two-three!"

"He'd better," someone said. "If the kids start throwing that ball around the field again, it'll be all over."

"Byrnes is too temperamental to suit me," a loud voice proclaimed. "Did you see the act he put on when Nickels let that wild pitch get away? Sure seems to think a lot of himself."

"A couple of major-league scouts seemed to think a lot of him," Collins countered.

"I think this guy acts like he's doing the game a favor by wearing a uniform with his name on the back. I'm a purist. A real ballplayer plays because he loves the game. I'm still waiting to see if Byrnes is more interested in what he can get out of the game than what he gives to the game."

"He's got everything," Collins said defensively. "Stands six-three, 190 pounds, has lots of speed, a good change-up, and a pretty good idea of where to put the ball. Anyway, when you're pitching with a gang of Fence Busters like this freshman bunch behind you—"

"You're right, Collins," another fan agreed. "This team's the best bunch of hitters I ever saw!" He pointed toward the left-field corner. "Say, Jim, how about that one warming up out there? Know him?"

Everyone in Collins's vicinity looked to the bullpen where a tall, slender youngster was beginning to throw.

Collins laughed. "Know him! You mean you don't? I thought everybody in this town knew Chip Hilton!"

"So that's Chip Hilton! Wonder why he isn't playing? From what I hear, he can do anything on a ballfield."

"I don't know about baseball," someone said knowingly, "but he can sure play football. Kicks, passes, runs. He was the key to the freshman team. He was almost like having another coach on the field."

"He didn't do bad in basketball either," someone added.

FENCE BUSTERS

"Just broke all the scoring records in the book," Collins said lightly. "In addition to winning the national shooting championship!"

"Why isn't he playing if he's so good?"

"That's what I've been trying to figure out," Collins replied. "All I can figure is that Rockwell doesn't want to be criticized for pushing his own players. Hilton pitched for the Rock at Valley Falls. Cohen and Morris were on the same team."

"How about Schwartz and Smith?"

"They played too!"

"Looks like he brought the whole team with him."

"That's what I mean. Rockwell doesn't want anyone to think he plays favorites."

"This game doesn't mean so awful much. Besides, look at the score. Seems like they could all play a little. Here we go! Varsity's got the big end of the stick up!"

The grandstand shadows reached home plate when Byrnes toed the rubber for his first pitch, and a strange stillness seemed to grip the fans. But only for a moment. Russ Merton, the varsity shortstop and leadoff man, fired up the crowd once again as he drilled Byrnes's fastball straight through the middle for a clean single. Byrnes made no play on the grounder, leaped nimbly aside, and watched the ball speed across second base and out to center field.

"See what I mean!" the loud-voiced fan yelled. "See what I mean!"

Merton drove for second base but retreated to first when Bob Emery, the freshman center fielder, came in fast and fielded the grass cutter. That put the tying run on first. But it didn't end there.

The next hitter, executing the obvious, pushed a slow roller to the right of the mound, and Byrnes fumbled the ball! Both runners were safe, and that put the winning run on base. But that still wasn't all! Byrnes threw his glove in disgust at the squirming ball, and the alert runners promptly and gleefully advanced another base before Biggie Cohen retrieved the ball. That put Merton on third and the push-along hitter on second. Rockwell called time!

The varsity players, scenting the kill, were out in front of their dugout now, riding Byrnes. Rockwell, Cohen, and Nickels surrounded the high-strung pitcher.

"Steady, Byrnes," Rockwell said gently. "Get a grip on yourself."

"I'm all right!" Byrnes shouted. "But where's my support?" He gestured toward the shortstop. "Morris should've had Merton's grounder!"

"The ball went right through your legs," Cohen said softly.

Byrnes glared angrily at Cohen. "The bunt was your play," he snarled.

Cohen was astonished. "My play!" he echoed. "It was right in front of you. I couldn't have fielded that ball if I'd been playing on top of the plate!"

"Enough!" Rockwell said sharply. "The damage is done. How do you feel, Byrnes? Can you finish it out? Do you want to finish it out?"

"Finish it out?" the angry pitcher growled. "Of course I want to finish it out!" He gestured toward Cohen. "That is, if I can get some help."

"All right. But if you don't feel up to it, say so. Hilton is ready!"

"Hilton!" Byrnes shouted, his face contorted with rage. "Hilton!" he repeated. "All I've heard since the first day of practice has been Hilton, Hilton, Hilton!"

CHAPTER 2

The Fireman Arrives

THE TRUE baseball fan wants to see the game played to the max, wants to see a player make a hard try for every ball and for every play. The fans knew the hotheaded hurler was solely responsible for the dangerous situation, and they resented his obvious attempts to shift the blame to Morris and Cohen. Byrnes, enraged, scarcely waited for Nickels's sign, threw too fast, and walked the third batter. That loaded the bases, and Rockwell again called time. While he was talking to the frustrated pitcher, the fans began to boo Byrnes and to second-guess Rockwell.

"Take him out!"

"Put in a real pitcher! Put in Hilton!"

"What are you waitin' for, Rockwell? Rain?"

"Who's coaching the team, you or the bat boy?"

Rockwell's eyes flickered toward the bullpen, but he decided against the impulse. The wily coach was trying to develop a pitcher; he was trying to help Byrnes find himself. The preseason series victory was unimportant if the big left-hander could be taught self-control. He delayed as long as possible before heading for the dugout. As he turned away, he said softly, "All right, Byrnes, put out your own fire."

Byrnes was on fire himself. He was angry with his teammates, the fans, Rockwell, and the varsity hitters. He fired the ball directly at the batter's head. It was a fastball, and only the swift slant of the speeding ball saved the hitter from disaster. But the blazing throw was too fast to evade the batter completely and careened off the cleanup hitter's shoulder. That brought an angry roar from the stands and sent the varsity charging for the mound. But the umpires, Rockwell, and Bennett got there first and broke up the melee.

The damage was done. When the field cleared, the umpire waved the batter to first, and Merton trotted across the plate with the tying run. It was the last of the ninth, the score tied at an unbelievable 29, the bases loaded, no one down, and the winning run on third.

Out in the bullpen, Chip Hilton and Soapy Smith had stopped throwing to watch the argument—what ballplayers call a "rhubarb." The two were lifelong buddies and formed an efficient battery. Hilton was a first-class hurler, solid in every respect. The tall, blond freshman had blinding speed, a wicked screwball, a good curve, and unusual control of a deceptive knuckleball. More importantly, he had poise, confidence, and self-control.

Chip's redheaded receiver was solid too. Smith had square shoulders and a sturdy frame, and the freckle-faced freshman had a strong arm. Base runners took few liberties when Soapy was behind the plate.

"That ties it up," Soapy said in disgust. "Now I suppose the Rockhead will give *you* a chance. Hah!"

The redhead was right. Rockwell turned at that very moment and waved them in. Then the veteran coach turned back to Byrnes. "That's all today," he said gently. "I'm sorry you did that."

Byrnes mouthed a curse and threw his glove clear across the diamond. The angry gesture drew another roar of disapproval from the crowd, and a chorus of boos and jeers accompanied the disgruntled pitcher as he stomped angrily to the dugout.

The walk from the bullpen to the mound is short or long, depending upon the situation and the traveler. Some baseball experts contend that a good relief pitcher is a special kind of athlete; he's the kind of pitcher who performs best when the odds are against his team and himself, who revels in the opportunity to wage the uphill fight. To the "fireman," the journey is routine, and the task is simply to get the job done—to just put out the fire.

Chip had plenty of confidence in his pitching ability and, like most athletes, preferred to be the underdog. But he was far from relaxed as he and Soapy trudged across the field. *I've got to do it,* he was thinking. *Just got to!*

Behind Chip's worry about the game and the series was his fondest hope for a good start for his high school coach, Henry Rockwell. And the big goal, the prize that would make Rock solid with the State fans, would be to win the preseason series with the varsity and then go on to win the Little Four championship. A & M, Tech, Cathedral, and State were bitter baseball rivals, and all were gunning for the title.

Chip wanted desperately to be a good college pitcher and to be a starter. He knew, too, that anyone who had played for Rock in high school would have to be twice as good as any of the other candidates. Chip grinned to himself. "This is a pretty good spot to prove I've got it," he murmured.

Soapy broke through his thoughts. "Just great! He waits until it's all over and then sends you in to take the heat. Just great!"

"What makes you think it's all over?" Chip chided.

Soapy squirmed. "Well, ah—" he hedged. "I didn't really mean it was over. I just couldn't help wondering why he waited so long. Why couldn't he use Dean? Why put you on the hot spot?"

"Because Dean's a lefty. Isn't it good strategy to throw in a right-hander when hitters have been looking at a southpaw all through the game?"

"Yes, but why wait so long? The crowd even got on him!"

Chip jabbed Soapy in the ribs. "Rock usually knows what he's doing, Soapy."

"I guess you're right, Chip," Soapy said uncertainly. Speed Morris joined them at the shortstop position near the edge of the grass.

"Tough assignment, man," he said grimly, "but you can do it!"

Biggie Cohen was next, walking beside Chip toward the rubber. "Rough, real rough, Chipper," he said, slapping Chip on the back. "But you've pulled us out of tougher spots. Just throw it in there! We'll back you up!"

Rockwell said nothing. He watched Chip begin his warm-up throws and then turned away. But Chip caught the whimsical smile that flashed across the Rock's lips, and that was enough for Chip. Words weren't too important where these two were concerned. Each believed in action and getting the job done.

"Hilton now pitching for the State Freshmen. Smith catching. Play ball!"

The varsity players started in on Chip where they'd left off on Byrnes. They crowded out of the dugout and issued their warning.

"Fresh meat, Reggie! Knock it down his throat!"

"C'mon, a bingle will do it!"

"Let's do it! We've played with these rookies long enough!"

Up in the grandstand, Jim Collins was excited. "You think Diston is good? Well, you just focus your eyes on this kid. Best *I* ever saw! Watch him!"

Chip was facing third base, the ball cradled at his waist between his glove and throwing hand. He pivoted quickly and blazed his fastball around Harris's knees on the inside.

"S-t-e-e-rike!"

Reggie Harris was a power hitter, and he took a full cut at every pitch, aiming for the fence. But Soapy called the pitches just right, low and inside, high and inside, and low and outside. Harris went down swinging on three pitches. Lee Carter tried too hard to be the hero. He forgot that a single was as good as a home run and popped-out to Biggie Cohen.

That made it two away, and the spectators abruptly reversed their stand, suddenly aware that they were watching a real sports drama. They realized the big kid out on the mound might conceivably perform the impossible. And just like that, they swung in line with Chip's teammates.

"Come on, Hilton, come on!"

"Atta baby! Set 'em down!"

Jaime "Minnie" Minson took his time selecting just the right bat, looked longingly at the left-field fence, and finally settled on a long, wooden thirty-eight-inch pole. Wrapping his big hands lovingly around the end of the heavy bat, down at the end, he stalked up to the third-base side of the plate. Minnie had decided to break up the ball game all by himself.

Chip came in with his blazing fastball, a streak of white that caught the inside corner between the wrists and the letters. Minson carefully looked over the called strike and then stepped away from the plate. He took a lot of time before he got back up there, expertly baiting the freshman pitcher.

Chip's change-up curve dropped low and outside to even the count, and Minson again backed out of the box. Once more he used all the time possible before pounding the plate and getting set. Chip grinned, and when Minson was firmly dug in, he stepped back off the rubber and off the mound.

That was the signal for the umpire to get into the act. He whipped off his mask and stepped out in front of the plate. "Time!" he shouted, slapping his cap across his thigh. "All right, you two. Now you listen to me! Both of you! Play ball and cut out this nonsense! Understand?" He glared from Minson to Chip and back again, replaced his mask, and walked quickly behind Smith. "Play ball!"

Chip toed the rubber and waited for Minson to get set. Facing third and watching the dancing runner, he slowly brought the ball down to his waist. Holding it there the full second, he suddenly stepped toward third and sent a sidearm, lightning-fast screwball around Minson's knees. It looked way outside, and Minnie hesitated a trifle too long. Then, too late, he thrashed his bat through with a mighty swing, fanning the breeze, and Chip was ahead one and two. Soapy called for a waste pitch. Chip responded with a wide, lazy curve that was high and outside.

FENCE BUSTERS

Minson really dug in then and got set for the certain fastball. The pitch had all the earmarks, the same overhand swing and fastball motion. But it was Chip's old dependable, his controlled knuckler. The blooper came twisting and bobbing down across Minson's shoulders. Minnie had started his swing but stopped and recovered his balance. But when he saw the ball heading for the strike zone, he tried to knock the cover off. All he hit was the dirt, the force of his empty swing spinning him around and down, a second after a smiling Soapy tossed the ball to the umpire.

The crowd roared, but Chip never heard the noise. He was hustling toward the dugout, trying to escape Biggie, Speed, and Soapy, who had him surrounded and were pounding him on the back and roughing him up as though he had won the game. Red Schwartz rushed out of the dugout and joined in the celebration.

Rockwell brought them back to reality. "Come *on*! Break it up! Let's get a hitter up there!"

Murph Gillen tossed away two of the three bats he'd been swinging and stepped into the batter's box. Determination was etched all over the powerful hitter's face. Murph nearly fooled everyone on the first pitch too. He dug in and faked a full swing before laying a slow roller down the third-base line. It was a beautiful bunt. But Minson made the perfect play, scooped up the ball with his throwing hand, and, in the same motion, whipped an underhand strike at first to nip the runner by a whisker. The fans applauded both players. It was good baseball.

Darrin Nickels didn't fool around. He put all of his 230 pounds behind his swing and laid the sweet spot of the bat against a high, rising fastball. The lofty fly carried clear to the center-field fence. But George Reed speared it, practically off the fence, for the second out.

Chip had been watching Rod "Diz" Dean warm up in the bullpen and expected Rockwell to send in a pinch hitter. But nothing happened, and so he walked up to the first-base side of the plate, accompanied by cheers from the fans and jeers from the varsity.

Ned Diston was the varsity's number-two pitcher, and he'd been invincible the previous year with a record of six victories and no defeats. He'd taken it easy with Gillen, but Nickels had scared him when he walloped the high waste pitch. Diston decided to bear down.

The first pitch came twisting in around Chip's wrists. It was a teaser. It looked fat coming in but broke at the last second. Chip started for it but checked his bat in time and stepped back.

"B-a-a-l-l."

In midmotion, Mitch "Widow" Wilder stopped his return to Diston and whirled around to face the umpire. "What?" he screamed. "Ball?" He gestured with the ball. "That was a ball?"

The varsity infielders came charging in too. "Ball?" they echoed. "Ball?"

The plate umpire wearily lifted his mask and pointed toward the field. "Get back out there and play ball!" he shouted. He calmly waved the testy fielders away and dusted off the plate, completely ignoring Wilder. The Widow might have been his shadow, yelling into the umpire's ear and shaking the ball in his face.

The fans loved it and got a big kick out of the argument, especially when the umpire straightened up, faced Wilder, and literally forced the big receiver away from the plate as they argued nose to nose. It was good fun and good strategy on Wilder's part. Wilder knew exactly what he was doing. He knew all about Chip Hilton from his high school days. He turned away from the umpire and started on Chip.

"You went through with the swing!" Widow shouted. "Bet you think you pulled a fast one, don't you? Humph! Real smart, fresh meat. Well, *that's* the last break you'll get." He gestured toward the umpire. "*He* won't let you get away with that again."

The umpire was in position now, his mask adjusted, and at the end of his patience. "Play ball or go to the bench."

Wilder played ball. He slowly pulled on his mask, squatted for the sign, and smugly glanced up to check out Chip's reaction to the special treatment. But he didn't get any satisfaction. Chip, oblivious to Wilder's attention, was concentrating on the pitcher out on the mound.

Diston shook off a sign and nodded for the next one. He wanted to try his screwball. The ball came in low and outside and caught the corner for a called strike. Chip never moved.

"Yeah!" Wilder jeered as he snapped the ball back to Diston. "We've got Mr. Timid here! Lookin' for the free ticket? Well, forget it, hero. We're strikin' you out!"

Diston shook Wilder off again and came in with the same pitch. And again Chip watched the ball go by.

"S-t-e-e-rike!"

Chip's stillness at the plate brought a barrage of advice from the fans.

"C'mon, kid, swing!"

"Hit away, big man. Nothing to lose—but the game!"

"Get that bat off your shoulder! Bang away!"

Chip waited outside the batter's box until Wilder whipped the ball back to Diston. Then he stooped for a bit of dust and rubbed the dry soil between both hands. He tried not to, but he found himself trying to figure the next pitch and attempting to outguess the pitcher. Diston would waste one now. He'd come in with something close just below the hands or down around the knees. "Then he'll come back with the screwball," Chip muttered as he stepped up to the plate.

Wilder, squatting in the catcher's box, tossed a spray of dirt over his shoulder, much to the disgust of the umpire. Then he looked up at Chip. "Talkin' to yourself, freshmeat? Don't like it, do you? Don't like the responsibility in the hot spot, do ya? Wait till we start levelin' off on you."

"C'mon, play ball," the umpire growled. "And the next time, you watch where you're throwing that dirt!"

The crowd hushed as Diston uncoiled and delivered the next pitch. The ball looked fat all the way in but dipped at the plate to spin down around Chip's knees, just missing the plate. Wilder, like all good catchers, was adept in covering the last-second flight of a ball at the plate. He did just that, covering and then edging glove and ball unnoticeably into the strike zone. He didn't move. He just waited with glove and ball poised knee-high over the inside corner of the plate.

Chip backed up confidently, but he breathed a little sigh of relief when he heard the umpire. "B-a-a-l-l!"

Diston and his teammates charged toward the umpire, and Del Bennett leaped out of the varsity dugout. But it was no good, the umpire held his ground, supported by the fans. They wanted action, and they were pulling for the blond hurler who'd put out the fire on defense to complete the game in a blaze of glory.

Collins's grandstand crowd was having a good time needling the big man.

"What's he waitin' for, Jim?"

"I thought you said he could hit!"

"That pitch looked good to me!"

"Good? It was right in there!"

"He can hit," Collins asserted. "Just wait."

CHAPTER 3

Swelling Occipital Bones

CHIP WAS waiting for the screwball. He watched Diston intently and was sure he'd figured it correctly when the big right-hander shook off Wilder's first sign. "Here it comes," he breathed.

Diston's overhand pitch came in around the letters, but the ball didn't spin away. It came whirling up as big as a pineapple and then flashed in and down under Chip's wrists, missing the plate by a foot. There wasn't any question about that one. It was way inside and brought the count to three and two.

Chip asked for time and stepped back out of the batter's box, completely disgusted with himself. How many times had Rock warned him about trying to guess the pitch, to outguess the pitcher? "Sucker," Chip muttered. "Plain, ordinary sucker!"

Diston waited until Chip was set and then gave the ball all he had. It came whistling in, and this time it was the screwball, the varsity star's favorite pitch. It came streaking in with all the signs of a three-two fast one. Chip's eyes focused on the ball, following its path right up to the plate. At the last second, it seemed, the fade-away darted toward the outside corner.

Chip was a pull hitter, a switch hitter who pulled the ball from either side of the plate. Batting against Diston, a right-hander, Chip ordinarily would have pulled to right or right center. And his pivot toward first base would have enabled him to cut down on the running time. But this time, he stepped toward the hot corner and put everything he had into a smooth, flowing swing, snapping his wrists through at the last second. The crack sounded like a rifle shot.

The power behind the blow carried Chip toward third base, but he pivoted quickly, regained his stride, and darted toward first in a desperate sprint. The dash carried him nearly to the bag before he realized the ball had winged its way straight for the left-field fence. Then, hearing the crowd roar, he fearfully turned his head to see the ball flying far over the left fielder's head and over the fence: a home run in any ballpark! All Chip had to do was touch all the bases!

That wasn't quite all. He still had to retire the varsity in the bottom of the tenth. One run wasn't much of an edge the way the upperclassmen had been slugging the ball.

Chip thought about that as he tagged each base. As he headed for home plate, he thought about one of Rockwell's hitting axioms: "Just meet the ball. Don't try to kill it!"

Chip could almost hear Rock saying, "The hitter who's always trying to knock the ball out of the park usually winds up watching the ball games from the dugout— watching the player who beat him out for a spot on the team hit the ball a mile just by meeting it."

Then Chip was mobbed at the plate, and he forgot all about outguessing the pitcher and trying to kill the ball. He was grinning happily when he ducked down into the dugout, but he didn't forget to urge the team to "go get some more runs." He flopped down on the bench and reached for his warm-up jacket. Then he heard the sneering voices, and he could hardly believe his ears.

"Glamour Boy Hilton, that's what they call him!"

"Sure is!"

"Must be nice to have your coach save you for the hero spots."

Lefty Byrnes, Darrin Nickels, and Ellis Burke were sitting a few feet away, side by side, their eyes fixed on the action out on the diamond. But their voices were cautiously lowered so the sound barely reached Chip's ears.

Chip was shocked speechless at the strange, unexpected attack. He glanced at Rockwell and his other teammates, but they obviously hadn't heard anything. They were cheering on Ozzie Crowell, urging him to "keep it going!"

Chip carefully adjusted the jacket around his arms and shoulders and tried to figure it out. Lefty Byrnes had received reams of publicity. And, as far as his teammates were concerned, the big southpaw had gained a tremendous amount of respect because of the fabulous bonus big-league scouts had reputedly offered him to sign a contract out of high school.

Chip didn't know much about Byrnes, except that the big pitcher was delivering pizzas at night to help pay his college expenses. But that was about all. Byrnes kept himself aloof from most of the freshman candidates. Darrin and Ellis were the only exceptions. Chip had never seen Byrnes with any of the other players, but he'd noticed that Nickels and Burke seemed proud to be friends with the star hurler.

SWELLING OCCIPITAL BONES

Darrin Nickels had been a little on the surly side the few times he'd worked behind the plate when Chip had been on the mound. Chip figured his friendship with Soapy might have been the reason. Everyone was hustling to make the team, and Soapy had looked exceptionally good in the early workouts. Nickels handled his 230 pounds almost as easily as Soapy Smith maneuvered his 200. But Nickels was superior with the bat. He powdered the ball and hit it a mile. But that was where the burly receiver's advantage ended. Soapy was a veritable workhorse. He hustled every second, chattered away a mile a minute, and kept the runners scared out of their wits with his laserlike pegs to the bases.

Ellis "Belter" Burke was another power hitter. The big left fielder knew how to get all of his 190 pounds into the swing of a bat. Burke had seemed all right to Chip up to this point. It didn't make sense.

"I don't get it," Chip was thinking. "I just don't get it!"

Ozzie caught a two-two fastball on the nose. But Diston speared it, leaping high in the air to pull in the hard-tagged ball, and retired the side with an easy toss to first.

The freshmen charged out on the field determined to hold the one-run lead, and the action temporarily shelved Chip's puzzlement over Byrnes, Nickels, and Burke.

The fans were fired up to the boiling point by this time, and they gave Chip another tremendous hand when he walked out to the mound. There was no doubt about the popularity of the blond hurler. The fans liked him. Jim Collins didn't have to sell this player. He'd sold himself.

"Set 'em down, kid! Set 'em down!"

"One-two-three! One-two-three, kid! One-two-three!"

"Three up and three down, kid! That's the plan!"

There were other reactions. Del Bennett, State's varsity coach, knew baseball, and he knew a major-league prospect when he saw one. Bennett was almost tempted to join in the applause. He liked the tall athlete. He liked the smooth windup, the graceful finish of his delivery, the way he rapped the ball, and, most of all, the kid's easygoing temperament. A hitting pitcher with poise and self-control was a rare find! His thoughts bounded back to the first time he'd seen Chip Hilton, when he'd been just one of hundreds of high school athletes who'd come to State to visit and learn about the university's educational facilities.

Bennett's eyes followed the sweep of Chip's long arm and the flash of lightning that streaked from his hand to Soapy's glove. The kid had it, all right! He'd earned it too. He'd dreamed of being a pitcher and had stuck to it. Hilton had been a first baseman on that visit, but he'd hung around until he got some college coaching on throwing a ball from the mound.

Bennett grinned at the recollection. The kid's friends had been that way, too, full of spirit and determination. Del's grin faded. It was too bad all kids couldn't be like them, too bad they couldn't play baseball to the max for the love of the game and still be good sports about it.

Bennett's eyes shifted to Biggie Cohen on first base. This big player was ready too—ready for the varsity or the big leagues. Del's old buddy, Stu Gardner, had been the first to tell him about Chip Hilton and Biggie Cohen. Stu had wanted his club to name these two for the upcoming minor-league draft when they graduated from Valley Falls High, but he had stepped aside when he learned they were interested in a college education first. Del Bennett heaved a deep sigh. "There ought to be more big-league scouts like Stu Gardner," he breathed.

"C'mon, Chipper, mow 'em down! Lay it in there, Chipper. We'll back you up!" Speed Morris, at his shortstop position, was pounding his glove and kicking up the dust with his spikes. Bennett smiled appreciatively. That was the spirit he liked to see!

"Give it to me, Chipper! Gimme a strike! Right down the alley! Can't hit 'em if they can't see 'em!" Soapy Smith's chanting drew Bennett's eyes. He sure remembered Smith. How could anyone forget the redheaded, freckle-faced comedian. Especially when he flashed the big smile that set his red freckles dancing.

Soapy's peg to second after Chip's last warm-up throw brought Bennett back to the business of baseball. He turned toward Wilder, who was waiting patiently at the bat rack. "OK, Wilder," he said sharply, "work him! You get on, and we'll push you around. I'm sending Jack King in to pinch hit for Diston. Lenny Harris is warming up in the bullpen. C'mon, now, we've got to get a run!"

Widow Wilder was real talkative behind the plate. The husky receiver supposedly talked to his pitcher, but his remarks were always directed to the batter—obvious attempts to "pull the hitter's chain." But Wilder could take lessons from Soapy Smith. He'd never been exposed to a line like Soapy's. Soapy started right in and reversed the big catcher's own tactics. The redhead had suffered silently when Wilder baited Chip earlier. Anyone who opposed Chip Hilton deserved all Soapy could dish out.

"Chip! Look who's here! The black widow herself! And no skirts! Chip, let's be nice. Throw it underhand! You know, women and children first and all that stuff."

Soapy squatted and gave the sign. Then, before Chip had time to toe the rubber, Soapy stepped across the plate in front of Wilder. "Excuse me, miss, ah, mrs., ah, ms., ah, just skip it!" He turned to the umpire. "Excuse me, sir, do you have a softer ball?"

The umpire glared angrily at Soapy. Then, without a word, he lifted the sleeve of his blue coat, and checking his watch, began to count the seconds. That did it! Soapy rushed back to his position with exaggerated haste, and Chip slipped a fastball across the plate for a called strike. Wilder was furious and eyed Soapy with rage. His grip on the bat was so tight he couldn't have hit a basketball.

Soapy ignored Wilder's angry glare and resumed his conversation with Chip. "*Now,* Chipper, that wasn't nice. Remember—remember how they let you hit the home run? C'mon, now, be a gentleman."

Chip wanted to strike Wilder out as much as he'd ever wanted to set anyone down. So he shook Soapy off until he got the pitch he wanted. Then he drifted a wide, sweeping curve to the outside corner, and Wilder missed it by a foot. Soapy held the ball in front of Wilder and turned it slowly in his hand. "This is it, Mr. Widow. This little round thing made from horsehide."

Chip and Soapy had the same idea on the next pitch: something close in and around Wilder's wrists. The screwball did the trick. It looked as if it was going to split the plate but sliced in and down under the angry catcher's elbows, and he never had a chance. Wilder had started his swing and couldn't stop, and the umpire called him out. Strangely enough, the Widow made no protest. He glared at the umpire and then gave Soapy a long look before stalking back to the varsity dugout. Soapy loved it!

Chip's infield teammates voiced their support. They chattered away.

"Atta baby, Chip!"

"That's the big one, Chip! Let me have number two!"

"Bear down!"

"Let 'em hit! We'll back you up!"

"Mow 'em down, Chip. Send 'em home!"

The infield chatter was great, but there the support ended. In the outfield, Ellis Burke in left, Bob Emery in center, and Murph Gillen in right leaned forward with their hands on their knees and were absolutely silent.

In the dugout, Lefty and Darrin watched Chip with smoldering eyes. They half hoped the varsity would knock him out of the box. Yet if anyone had asked these five players why, they couldn't have given a single logical reason for their dislike of Chip Hilton.

A sports psychologist could write a few papers on the problem. Lefty Byrnes, the star pitcher, had simply been bitten by the "green-eyed monster" and had used his influence to poison the minds of his friends and admirers. Byrnes had turned his group against Chip because of his own petty jealousy.

Gil Mack had played up Chip's all-around athletic ability several times and had even written a special story about the Valley Falls star for the Sunday magazine section of the *Herald*.

In every group and on every team, challengers emerge seeking leadership. Chip Hilton possessed the right qualities. He was personable, modest, sufficiently aggressive, and a fine athlete. He had a quiet confidence in his ability to meet each situation as it came, and he was a gentleman. He was a natural.

Lefty Byrnes had all the physical qualities, but he'd been spoiled by too much praise and adulation. Fame had come too early, and he foolishly believed everything he read about himself. Some athletes can read their press clippings and forget all the adjectives. Byrnes wasn't the type. The big left-hander was afflicted with the difficulty that often attacks young athletes with too much ego. Knute Rockne, Notre Dame's immortal football coach, used to describe this affliction as "a swelling of the occipital bones."

Chip tried to forget the words he'd heard in the dugout as the next hitter came to the plate. He'd expected Del Bennett to send in a pinch hitter for Diston, and he sized up his next opponent carefully.

Jack King stood about five-nine and looked to be built of granite. Chip had never seen the pinch-hitting outfielder before, but he saw that King had all the marks of a natural hitter.

King walked confidently up to the first-base side of the plate and dug in at the back of the batter's box. He poised his bat steadily over his shoulder and stared at Chip with keen, steady eyes. It was impossible to miss his businesslike approach. He was serious and had better be treated that way.

Soapy had measured the hitter too. And, like Chip, Soapy knew that here was a real hitter. Soapy squatted and gave Chip the sign for a fastball. Chip promptly shook him off, sensing that King liked the fast ones. Soapy then called for a curve, and Chip settled for that, sending in a sharp, darting curve around King's wrists. It was close, but the umpire called it a ball. Chip came right back with the same pitch and again the ump called, "B-a-a-l-l!" Now Chip was behind in the count, and the varsity players really opened up for their teammate.

Chip sized up King again and once more decided against the fastball. He passed up the blooper, too, and settled for the screwball. The pitch came in fast toward King's wrists and then split the plate knee-high. Jack waited that one out, and the count was two and one.

SWELLING OCCIPITAL BONES

Chip kept shaking off Soapy's signs until the call was for the blooper. He faked his fastball and sent the high-looping knuckler in toward the strike zone. It seemed almost as if King was waiting for the pitch because he made no false motion; he simply waited until the ball dropped into hitting distance and then leveled off. There was a sharp crack as King golfed the ball high into the air toward the short right-field fence.

Murph Gillen had started in fast but reversed his path when he saw the ball was hit harder than it appeared. It should have been an easy out, but the bad start was too much of a handicap, and the ball dropped behind Gillen and rolled to the fence. King skipped around first and held up at second, and the tying run was in scoring position.

Russ Merton was an ideal leadoff man. The five-seven shortstop crowded the plate, had a good eye, and was a consistent .300 hitter. Chip evened the count at two and two, and then Merton topped the ball, sending it weakly along the third-base line. Crowell came up with it but threw wildly to first, pulling Cohen off the bag.

Biggie was lucky to stop the ball, but he scooped it up and fired it right back to third base where Morris was covering. It was a perfect clothesline throw and it had King by a mile, but Speed dropped the ball! Jack King gleefully slid into the base, and Russ Merton scampered safely down to second. The winning run was on second base, and the varsity was tearing down the dugout.

In the freshman dugout, Darrin Nickels lowered his head and grinned when Lefty Byrnes nudged him with his elbow. "Here he goes," Nickels said softly.

"It doesn't make me mad," Byrnes whispered.

Up in the grandstand, the crowd around Collins was pulling for the freshmen Fence Busters, but that didn't stop the fans from heckling Jim.

"Same old thing," someone remarked. "Good hit, no field!"

"Your blond wonder pitcher doesn't seem to be doin' so good!"

Jim Collins turned to face the speaker. "You can't blame Hilton for the errors," he said defensively. "He can't do everything!"

"They hit the ball, didn't they?"

Collins shrugged. "If you call that hitting the ball, you don't know much about baseball."

Chip delivered four straight balls. Soapy stepped out of the catcher's box each time to catch the wide pitches. Chip was purposely loading the bases, giving the varsity push-along hitter, Ted "Tubby" Ryder, an intentional pass and setting up a play at any base.

A grandstand heckler nudged a seatmate and directed a remark toward Jim Collins. "If this Hilton is so good," he said roughly, "let's see him scramble out of this mess!"

CHAPTER 4

Grandstand Play

INSIDE BASEBALL always intrigues the baseball fan. Vital game decisions provide him with wonderful opportunities to second-guess the big-league manager or the college coach. Critical game situations and demanding snap-judgment decisions develop in sandlot pickup games as often as they do in major-league parks. That's one of the many reasons baseball is the national game.

The situation developing in the last frame of the hectic contest between State's varsity and freshman teams was exactly what the fans wanted: bottom of the tenth, the varsity at bat, one run behind, one down, and bases loaded!

The opinions in the grandstand and the bleachers flew fast and furious.

"It's a tough spot!"

"Especially with the number-three hitter up and the cleanup guy on deck!"

"They'll hit away!"

"No way. It'll be the squeeze."

"Bentley and Reed are good hitters. One of the two will hit the ball. That's for sure!"

"Could be! But suppose Bentley hits the ball on the ground and into a double play? The game will be over, and Del Bennett will get the blame for losing the game."

"So what? He gets paid, doesn't he?"

"What's that got to do with it? He wants to win!"

"Who doesn't?"

"Well, then he'll squeeze in the tying run. And if Bentley is thrown out at first, so what? The game will be tied up, and Reed can win the game with any kind of a hit."

"Sounds good."

Standing behind the mound, his glove under his arm, Chip was rubbing the ball between his bare hands. But he was doing something else, he was doing some pitcher thinking. Given past situations, it had to be the squeeze. At that moment, Rockwell called time and joined Chip and Soapy and the entire infield. The players waited quietly for Rock's decision.

"Their only play is the bunt," Rockwell said decisively. "Bennett will play it safe and play for the tying run. We'll move in and stop the play at the plate! OK?"

"Right," Biggie said quickly. "Right!"

"It's up to you guys," Rockwell said gently. "Make them earn it!"

Bentley made a great show of digging in, squirming his spikes in the ground, and swishing his bat through in a full swing. But the act meant nothing to Chip and the infielders. They were playing for the bunt even if Bentley knocked the ball down their throats.

Chip came in with a high fastball, but Bentley never moved. He had evidently been told to "take one."

"B-a-a-l-l!"

Chip decided he'd slip the next one into the strike zone. He wasn't going to get too far behind. The varsity players were out in front of their dugout and greeted the umpire's call with a boisterous cheer. They followed that with a barrage of hoots and advice for Bentley.

"Make him pitch, Bill! A walk is as good as a hit!"

"Wait him out, Billy boy! You've got him worried."

"Here you go, Billy! Send him to the showers!"

Chip heard them. Alone on the mound, the pitcher hears his teammates and the opposing players and the crowd—and especially the baseball critic with the foghorn voice who never misses any game and always sits in the same seat. The hurler hears a lot until he gets the sign, goes into his motion, and concentrates on the strike zone.

Chip knew Bentley wasn't going to go for a bad one. *A walk is as good as a hit.* As good? Better! Well, Chip Hilton wasn't going to issue a free pass to this batter.

Soapy called for a curve, and Chip came in with the pitch, catching the outside corner around the batter's knees. The umpire's right hand shot up in the air, and that evened the count at one and one. Chip felt better.

Jack King was dancing away from third, and Tubby Ryder was scuffing up the dirt close to first. But neither strayed very far from the base. They were playing it safe, but not Russ Merton. Merton was taking a big lead, practically daring Chip to trap him between second and third. Soapy called for a fastball, and Chip nodded.

Toeing the rubber and facing third, Chip glanced toward the plate for Soapy's target. It took all his control to still the start of surprise when Soapy flashed the sign for the pickoff play. Cold sweat broke from Chip's forehead. He had nearly moved and might have committed a balk.

Chip counted to three and turned his head slowly from third to second. Yes, Speed had caught Soapy's signal and darted behind Merton. The throw would have nailed the stocky player by a mile if the wily little veteran had tried to get back to the bag.

But Merton hadn't even moved when Morris sprinted for the sack. Russ would have kept going toward third to draw the throw, and King would have dashed for home. That would have meant at least two and maybe three throws, and the way the team had been throwing the ball around, anything might happen. No, Chip wasn't going to risk it. He felt a twinge of regret when he noted the hurt expression on Soapy's face and the surprised look Speed flashed in his direction.

Chip shook his head regretfully and then put everything he had into his fastball. The runners broke with the delivery, and King was leading the way. The squeeze was on!

It was beautiful to watch! Bentley whirled and leveled his bat in the bunt position, and at the same time, Chip, Biggie, Durley, Morris, and Crowell sprinted forward as if pulled by the same string. The ball flashed straight for the center of the strike zone, shoulder-high, and Bentley plopped a perfect spinner in fair territory six feet to the left of the plate.

Chip was a step ahead of King and dashing for the whirling ball. One agonized glance told him Soapy could never make the play, and Durley was too far behind the runner. Soapy couldn't reach the ball, but he leaped forward and crouched in front of the plate. King would sure have to bowl Soapy over to score that run.

It looked like a certain tally, and the varsity exploded with a mighty cheer. Then Chip made his move, diving for the ball just as King started his slide. Chip hurtled through the air just as if he was executing a diving roll block on the football field.

What happened next was difficult to follow. Chip's spinning body tumbled into King, and the two flying bodies sprawled in a tangle of legs and arms in front of the plate. But the ball was in Chip's hand, and the precious sphere was pressed tightly against King's left ankle.

Soapy leaped aside at the last instant, and the umpire took his place. Standing astride the plate, the ump caught the full force of the plunging bodies and was cut down in the play. But his right hand was held high in the air with the thumb pointing over his shoulder, and that well-known gesture brought a tremendous roar from the crowd. The runner was out!

Chip tossed the ball to Soapy and called time. When he scrambled to his feet, a terrific burst of applause broke from the stands. And the fans kept it up, cheering and stomping their feet in a continuous thunder of approval. Jim Collins was jumping up and down like a little boy and yelling at the top of his lungs, and the expert who didn't like Lefty Byrnes was still at it, still making comparisons. "See the difference between Hilton and Lefty Byrnes!" he shouted. "See what I mean? See? Did you see?"

Lefty Byrnes and Darrin Nickels had leaped to their feet and were leaning over the apron of the dugout to watch the action. Byrnes was green with envy. "Grandstand play," he sneered. "Grandstander!"

"It was a great play," Nickels said grudgingly. "I don't know how he did it!"

Rockwell rushed out onto the field and pushed through the circle of players who had surrounded Chip. He clamped Chip's arm. "You all right, Chipper?" he asked anxiously. "You sure you're all right?"

Chip grinned and nodded. "Sure, Coach," he said lightly. "I'm all right."

Biggie Cohen laughed. "All right!" he repeated. "All right! I'll say he is! Never better!"

Jack King was pretty badly shaken up, but he patted Chip on the back before he turned for the varsity dugout. "Nice going—even for a freshman," he said ruefully. "You sure surprised me! I didn't even see you coming."

Del Bennett had been halfway to the plate and ready to launch a protest, but King's sportsmanship made him change his mind. "What a play!" he muttered in admiration.

The stands were still buzzing when the plate umpire called,"Play ball!" and Chip again faced the plate. It was two away now, and the freshman infield was playing deep, ready for a play at any base for the third and final out and the victory! Not that the freshmen felt the game was in the bag. No, they had too much respect for George Reed. The varsity cleanup hitter had hit four for four so far in the game. No, this game wasn't in the bag by a long shot. The varsity certainly wasn't throwing in the towel with the bases loaded and a hitter like Reed at bat.

A big right-hander, Reed carried his bat high. Chip kept the ball low and inside. The big center fielder passed up the first three pitches and then fouled off three straight. Again, on the full count with two out and bases loaded, the runners moved with Chip's delivery. It was another screwball around the knees, and Reed got solid wood on it!

This time, the ball was fair, a white streak that the fans never saw. But they did hear two loud cracks, two distinct cracks! And they saw Chip Hilton spin clear around with an extended glove and keep on turning and then run toward the dugout. On the way, they saw him smile and toss the ball to his coach, Henry Rockwell.

Then the fans saw the umpire's arm extended over his head, with his thumb pointing over his shoulder, and they knew the game was over. They realized then that the blond hurler must have snared a ball that had been hit so hard they never even saw it leave the bat! And they realized the freshmen had won the first game of the pre-season series, beating the varsity. A bunch of newcomers had beaten the conference champions.

Gee-Gee Gray was talking into his headset mike a mile a minute. Gray had caught Gil Mack's excitement and was as enthusiastic about the Fence Busters as the student sportswriter was.

"I never saw the ball, but I do know Hilton caught it because the force of the ball whirled him clear around, and he kept right on toward the dugout with it in his glove. It was a great catch, but the play, *the* play was the second out, that play at the plate! That play, fans, was one of the greatest I've ever witnessed. Chip Hilton, the freshman pitching and hitting sensation of this game, dove for the ball—he picked it up as he turned in the air—and then crashed into King with a perfect roll block, knocking Jack's foot away from the plate *and* tagging him with the ball while he was spinning through the air.

"If I live to be a thousand, I won't see that play duplicated. This kid is sensational! I've seen hundreds of sensational plays during the years I've been bringing you State sports, but the thriller of a lifetime—that play—was *it*. And I mean it!

"This kid, Chip Hilton, has already established himself in my book as one of the brightest athletes to ever enter State University. I'm sure I've got lots of company. I've got lots of company right now. Just listen to the hand this kid is getting!

FENCE BUSTERS

"Just in case you're wondering why there's such a crowd here today, let me explain. This freshman team is the most publicized group to ever represent the university.

"State students and university residents are wild about football, and everyone in this part of the state catches backboard fever during the hardcourt season. But baseball is *the* game that holds the fans year-round—Little League, spring training, farm teams, the regular season, inter-league play, the World Series, and even international games and the Olympics. Yes, baseball is the year-round pastime! And there are no more loyal baseball fans in the world than those right here in State University.

"To get back to the reason for the big crowd gathered here to see this first game of State's preseason series, the varsity is a veteran team and the conference champs, but the kids, the Fence Busters, have stolen their thunder and gotten all the publicity. They've certainly caught the fancy of the fans, and the varsity veterans don't like it.

"Yes, sir, Babe Ruth, Hank Aaron, Sammy Sosa, and Mark McGwire made baseball history because they were sluggers. These kids are sluggers too. They proved that today. And they also proved that the advance publicity about their hitting ability was not sports hype. The varsity doesn't like all that sports glory focused on the new-comers to State's sports scene, and quite a feud has developed. This afternoon the kids added insult to injury by slugging through a thrill-packed game to take the lead in the series. Well, folks, it clearly wasn't a defensive low-run battle, but it *was* a battle with a wild score.

"You better get out here early Friday afternoon. Now for the stats of this long slug-fest—"

The crowd had swarmed out on the diamond, and as the spectators moved slowly toward the parking lots and gym, the name of Chip Hilton was on the lips of every fan. Jim Collins had picked up some new listeners and was telling them all about Chip Hilton and the Fence Busters.

Lefty Byrnes and Darrin Nickels trudged silently along with the crowd in the direction of the gym. Ahead they could see a cluster of fans and players packed solidly around Chip, trying to pat him on the back and still showering him with their praises.

Emery, Burke, and Gillen waited by the gate, and the three outfielders fell in beside Byrnes and Nickels. The faces of the disgruntled five hardly expressed what one would expect after such a brilliant victory.

"What is this?" Gillen growled. "A one-man team?"

"It looks like it," Bob Emery muttered.

"Maybe we better turn in our uniforms," Burke said savagely.

"Putting on a real show, isn't he?" Nickels sneered bitterly.

"You'd think he won the game all by himself," Gillen said.

Byrnes was glowering at Chip's back. "I'll fix him," he promised. "Wait and see!"

CHAPTER 5

A Precious Gold Baseball

MITZI SAVRILL had been watching the door for fifteen minutes. From the cashier's desk at Grayson's, Mitzi had a clear view of the street as well as the entire store, especially the fountain and food area—much to the delight of Soapy Smith. When Chip and Soapy rushed in, fresh out of the shower and fresh out of breath from hurrying to get to work on time, Mitzi glanced pointedly at the clock. Soapy caught the message and stopped to explain, but Chip hurried on to his storeroom duties. Outwardly, Soapy was deeply apologetic. Secretly, he was delighted to have the opportunity to talk to the light of his life.

"It was a ten-inning game, with lots of runs, Mitzi, and we won! We beat the varsity! I mean Chip did!"

"You know what they say about all play and no work—"

"We'll make up for it, Mitzi! Honest!"

The stern expression on the cashier's face softened. "I was only kidding," she said sweetly. "Congratulations!"

A PRECIOUS GOLD BASEBALL

Her violet-blue eyes followed Chip's hurrying figure. "To both of you," she added softly.

Soapy made it to the storeroom, somehow. Entering in a daze, he took off his windbreaker, hung it up, took it down again, put it on, and started for the door.

"Hey!" Chip called. "Where you going? The fountain, the counter, remember? You work here!"

"Oh, yeah," Soapy replied. "She's wonderful!"

"So is State and getting an education and having a good job where *you* can watch the love of your life every night and having a boss like George Grayson who lets you play baseball and still draw a paycheck every week. Paycheck! Get it? Money! It pays for college bills—"

Soapy interrupted. "And candy and flowers! Sweets for the sweetest. Sure, I get it! See you later!"

Chip followed Soapy to the door and watched him move behind the counter. Soapy was the most popular Grayson's employee. Fred "Fireball" Finley shared the counter duties with Soapy and seemed oblivious to Soapy's approach until the addled catcher was just behind him. Then, Fireball deftly thrust out a leg and tripped his coworker.

"What's that for?" Soapy demanded indignantly. "Didn't I win the game? Didn't I uphold the honor of the freshman class? Where would guys like you be if it wasn't for great ballplayers like me, huh? Where? Tell me."

Fireball regarded Soapy gravely. "First, you tell me how guys like you could play baseball if it wasn't for guys like me."

Soapy's mood changed instantly. "I'm sorry, Fireball," he said. "I didn't really mean that. I really appreciate the extra work you're doing so I can play. I'll make it up somehow, honest!"

Fireball grinned. "I was kidding, Soapy. You know that! Skip it! You might try waiting on a few customers

43

though. I'm bushed. Seems like everybody on the campus wanted frosteds or sundaes or one of your weird specialties. Maybe it's spring!"

Soapy glanced across toward the cashier's desk and sighed. "I know," he said mournfully. "I know. Hey, how's your new heartthrob?"

Finley playfully punched Soapy in the ribs. "She's really special, Soapy," he said earnestly. "Her dad's a great guy too."

"You're telling me! He loves baseball! You should've heard him at the game. I could hear him over everyone else. He's some fan!"

"Maybe too much of a fan."

Soapy bridled. "How can anyone be too much of a baseball fan?" he demanded indignantly.

"Well, he's got a few responsibilities besides baseball, you know."

"Cynthia?"

"Of course. It costs a lot of money to put a girl through college, and running a big farm is no joke."

Finley's serious attitude sobered Soapy instantly. The two could have been brothers except Fireball was bigger and better looking. He had red hair and blue eyes, and packed 210 pounds on his six-foot frame. Soapy winked an eye knowingly as he put an extra scoop of ice cream in the blonde's hot fudge sundae.

"You're really serious about her, aren't you?" he asked. "Right?"

Fireball nodded. "That's for sure!"

"Well, look cool," Soapy warned. "Here she comes and with her dad too!"

Jim Collins headed straight for Soapy. "Congratulations, Smith! Great game! Where's Hilton? In the storeroom? Think it's all right to go on back? I've just got to

shake hands with that one. I'll be right back, Cindy."
Cynthia didn't even hear her father. She and Fireball
were talking in low voices, their heads close together and
oblivious to everyone.

Chip was seated at the storeroom desk, working on
the computer and perpetual inventory spreadsheets,
when Collins knocked and opened the door. "Hi ya, Chip!
What a game! Every fan in town is talking about you! I'm
hosting a barbecue for the whole team at my house
tomorrow right after practice. Can you make it?"

Chip shook his head. "I'm sorry, Mr. Collins. I have to
work. Besides, I've got a lot of studying to do. Working,
baseball, and hitting the books keep me hopping."

Collins was visibly disappointed. "Well, that's too
bad, Chip. I was really counting on having the whole
team there, especially you." The big man lingered a little
longer, trying to convince Chip that he ought to come for
a little while. Cynthia could drive Chip in from the farm
right after dinner. In the end, Collins regretfully gave up
and made Chip promise he'd come out to the farm some
Sunday after church.

Soapy was busy behind the counter. He was trying to
serve everyone in sight so Fireball would have time to
talk to Cindy. But busy as he was, Soapy kept one of his
big ears cocked in Fireball's direction. Soapy could tell
Fireball was excited about something because he was
speaking too fast and a little too loud.

"Why invite the whole team? Why does he have to do
things like that? Especially when you have to do all the
work."

"But I'm not doing all the work. Aunt Mary will over-
see most of the details. Besides, she always brings a few
of her friends to make sure everything's covered. Anyway,
it isn't work; it's fun!"

"That's what I'm getting at—"

"Don't tell me you're jealous! Why don't you come too?"

"I'm not jealous, but I am worried about . . . well, about the farm."

Cindy's face clouded, and there was a short silence. Then Fireball said contritely, his voice filled with concern, "I'm sorry, Cin. I didn't mean to say that."

"That's all right, Fireball, but I really wish you'd come. We could have a lot of fun."

"But I'm not on the team, and your father didn't invite me."

"I invited you. Besides, you're a better baseball player than anyone on the team. You didn't make the all-state baseball team just because you played quarterback on the football team!"

That remark brought Soapy from silent listener to instant interrogator. "You mean you were an all-state ballplayer?" he demanded.

Finley was surprised, but he always had a comeback for Soapy. "My, but what big ears you have, Soapy," he said grimly.

Soapy wiggled his ears appreciatively. "The better to hear you with, my darling," he said smugly. Then he remembered. "Hey, you never told me you played baseball!"

Finley raised an eyebrow in mock surprise. "Did I have to?"

"You tell me everything else."

Cindy was fingering the gold baseball on the thin gold chain around her neck. "He was all-state for two years," she said proudly, "and he turned down a pro contract to come to college—from the Eagles!" Finley was uncomfortable. "It didn't mean anything," he said, shrugging his shoulders.

The blonde broke up the conversation. "Since when does a hot fudge sundae have butter pecan ice cream in it?" she demanded.

Soapy was deeply apologetic. "These new scoops have been causing us all sorts of trouble!" he explained. He reached into his pocket and produced a card. "Permit me to give you a rain check on your next guzzle fuzz," he said, bowing and placing the card on the counter.

"Why do you have the telephone number printed so large?" the blonde asked innocently.

"So your big beautiful eyes can read it easily," Soapy rejoined, smiling. "Especially big brown eyes."

Finley began to sing in a low voice, "Five feet two, eyes of blue—"

Soapy cast a demoralized glance toward the cashier's desk and pivoted sharply away from the pretty customer. "Please, Mr. Finley," he hissed. "Hush!"

Soapy ignored the blonde completely after Finley's warning, but his sharp eyes noted that she picked up the card. Fireball noticed that too. After Collins and Cynthia left, Fireball began talking in a voice that carried clear across the store about employees who presented customers with their name cards.

"Please, Fireball," Soapy pleaded, "she'll hear you."

"That's what you get for eavesdropping," Fireball growled.

"I'll never do it again. Promise! And I won't tell what you were talking about either!"

Soapy broke part of the promise that very night. But he felt the end justified the means. Soapy was afraid he'd hurt Fireball's feelings, and he really appreciated Fireball taking the early shift week after week. Soapy decided to talk to Chip about Fireball.

Chip had the responsibility of closing the store and checking the inventory spreadsheets each night, and Soapy always waited for his friend. On the way home to Jefferson Hall, they talked baseball. Chip was surprised to find out Finley had been an all-state ballplayer.

"I'll bet he's been suffering all through spring practice," Chip said gravely. "How about that! All the time we were working out, he was coming in early and covering our work."

"*Our* work!" Soapy remonstrated. "You mean *my* work!"

"Same thing."

"It doesn't have a thing to do with your job. You know something? Fireball's changed completely since the football trouble you and he had. He never said a thing about being a good player when we were talking baseball. That's some change from the guy who talked about nothing except Fireball Finley when we first met him."

"I wish I'd known," Chip said. "I wouldn't have let him talk me into going out for the team."

"His job has nothing to do with—"

"Oh, yes, it has! Remember there's two of us away from the job. We'll just have to make it up to him someway, that's all."

Soapy stopped suddenly. "I know one way," he said excitedly. "It's not much, but it will help. He'd like to go to the Collinses' for the team barbecue tomorrow night."

"That's easy," Chip said cheerfully. "I can work at the counter until he gets back. I'm way ahead on my work. We'll tell him tonight, OK?"

Jeff was an extremely democratic dormitory. Maybe because many of the Jeffs had part-time jobs on or off campus. That may have been the bond that made Jeffs so loyal to one another and so proud of their dorm. Still, the rooms at Jeff were small. There wasn't much space for anything except standard dormitory furniture, and each room was assigned to two students. Yet each cubicle had a definite personality. Perhaps because the posters hanging on the walls and the bulletin boards in most of the rooms were filled with photos of friends and family. Also, perhaps because the bright curtains and colorful bedspreads moms had sent provided a touch of home for their sons.

Room 212 on the second floor was furnished simply enough but was one of the most popular rooms in the building. The magnet was a strange combination of leadership and prankish fun. Chip Hilton, the president of Jeff, and Soapy Smith, the clown prince of the dorm, lived in 212. Chip was elected unanimously last fall to the important post. Soapy just moved in and took charge of the fun for everyone in the place. Soapy was that kind of guy.

Room 212 was crammed as soon as the two roommates turned on the light. It seemed to Chip that the whole dorm was trying to get into the room to congratulate him on the big victory. Nobody listened to his protests that he'd done nothing. He was a Jeff man and he'd won the game; he was the hero, and that was all there was to it! Chip liked it, of course. Who wouldn't? But it made him uncomfortable, and he was glad when his admirers trooped off to bed.

Biology lab kept Chip late the next afternoon, and practice was well underway when he arrived. Rockwell was belting long flies to the outfield, and the pitchers were limbering up in front of the grandstand.

Soapy was waiting with his big glove, and Chip began to loosen up. Lefty Byrnes was throwing to Nickels nearby, and their sarcastic chuckles and low-voiced references to the Rock and the "wonder boy" brought Chip back to the problem yesterday's game had revealed. He was glad Jim Collins had managed to get Henry Rockwell to agree to a short practice so the guys could get out to the farm on time.

Later, at Grayson's, he forgot the whole thing as Fireball Finley flashed a grateful smile to him and Soapy and took off for the Collins farm.

Mitzi Savrill had clipped the little blurb about the barbecue from the school paper, and Soapy brought it over for Chip to read. Jim Collins was on the sports page again.

JIM COLLINS PLAYS HOST TO FRESHMAN BASEBALL SQUAD

Members of the colorful freshman baseball squad are celebrating their recent victory with a barbecue this evening at the Collins farm. Jim Collins, a local baseball booster, has invited the players, managers, and Coach Henry Rockwell.

The Collins farm is one of the prettiest in the county and has been the scene of many such events in the past. Jim is known to every baseball player who has worn a State uniform during the past twenty years, and the current freshman stars will get a terrific lift from the evening.

Few of the present-day baseball stars know it, but Jim Collins was one of the greatest diamond performers ever to play baseball in this part of the state. In fact, State baseball and Jim Collins are usually mentioned in the same breath by local fans.

A PRECIOUS GOLD BASEBALL

A note of caution: Take it easy on all that great food, freshmen. You're playing the varsity tomorrow afternoon, and the upperclassmen have sworn tomorrow's game will be nothing like the last one. They're out to avenge yesterday's defeat! A word to the wise.

Soapy grunted, "Humph! We'll kill 'em!"

CHAPTER 6

Lessons in Baseball

SOAPY WAS intrigued. He listened quietly as Finley described the inscription Jim Collins had placed over the fireplace in the big farmhouse's living room.

"God bless our mortgaged home," Soapy repeated. "That's good! He must have a wonderful sense of humor."

"It isn't funny," Finley said shortly. "He's in debt up to his ears, and Cindy is worried about the mortgage payments. She's thinking about dropping classes and going to work."

"He wouldn't let her do that."

"What could he do?"

Soapy spread his hands in a helpless gesture. "You got me, pal. Couldn't he work in University and on the farm?"

"And give up baseball? Not him! All he thinks about is balls and strikes and hits and the old days. To listen to him, he was the best catcher who ever pulled on a mask."

"Maybe he was!"

"Oh, sure!"

"How big did you say the steaks were?"

"About the size of home plate!"

"Mmmmmm. You have a good time?"

"Sure did! Thanks to you!"

"And Chip," Soapy added.

Finley paused. "That reminds me," he began. "Did Chip ever have any trouble with Byrnes?"

Soapy hesitated and shook his head slowly. "I guess you couldn't call it trouble," he said. "Byrnes made a couple of sarcastic remarks to Chip, but that's all."

"Well, anyway," Finley continued, "everything was going great until after the meal. Byrnes said he'd have to leave—he delivers pizzas. Mr. Collins said it was too bad guys like Chip and Byrnes have to work, and then he said something about Chip being a clutch player. Byrnes sort of laughed then and said anyone could be a star if the coach saved him for the right spot. It looked like trouble for a minute. You know Biggie!"

Soapy nodded. He knew Biggie Cohen, all right— knew that anyone who started anything with Chip Hilton was stepping on Biggie's big toes, and that meant trouble. Soapy grinned. "Yeah, I know. What happened?"

"Well, nothing much. Biggie started toward Byrnes, but Nickels and Morris moved in between them, and Nickels whispered something to Byrnes. Then his crew all piled into the pizza-mobile and left. Mr. Collins was puzzled, but Cindy smoothed it over by asking him to tell about the time he badgered a pitcher he was catching into throwing a no-hitter."

Soapy was all ears. "A no-hitter? How? How'd he do it?"

"Well," Fireball continued, "it sounds like this pitcher had a lot of stuff but no confidence. So Mr. Collins got the idea of kidding this guy into believing he was terrific. He kept telling him how fast he was and how the fastball he was throwing was so hard that Collins's glove hand had swelled up so big he couldn't get it out of his glove.

"So, in an important championship game, this pitcher was on the mound, and Collins began giving him the buildup. The other team couldn't get a hit, and this pitcher began to get a swelled head, and so Collins starts to bear down on him, telling him he's a quitter and that the manager is going to pull him if he doesn't start to pitch. This goes on for a few innings, and the pitcher is fit to be tied. He wants to murder Collins. Still, Collins keeps it up, and the guy is so mad at him that he pitches a no-hitter."

Fireball was enjoying Soapy's concentration. He grinned and continued, "That is, if you can believe my future father-in-law."

"What!" Soapy shouted, breaking the number-one library rule and drawing a militant glare from the librarian. "Do you mean you're engaged?"

"*Shhhh.* I'm just kidding. You want me to tell you the rest of the story or not?"

"Sure, but—"

"No *buts*! Anyway, the upshot of the whole thing was that the pitcher didn't know Collins was messing with his mind until after the game, and then they became fast friends. You like fish stories, Soapy?"

Soapy didn't answer. He was deep in thought. Fireball's story had given him an idea, and Soapy toyed with it through History 102 and during the long afternoon while he was sitting in the bullpen.

Alumni Field was jammed, and the Fence Busters took it in stride by getting off to a good start once again.

Ozzie Crowell hit the first pitch of the ball game right back at the pitcher. The ball flew past pitcher

LESSONS IN BASEBALL

Lenny Harris's legs, over second, and on out into center field. Speed Morris laced a liner into right field and went on to second when varsity's right fielder, Lee Carter, made the long, futile throw to third in an attempt to nip Crowell.

Bob Emery, a left-handed hitter, caught one of Harris's port-side curve balls right on the nose and pulled it straight as a string to the right-field fence. Crowell and Morris scored, and Emery held up at second. Then Biggie Cohen, playing the role of cleanup hitter according to the script, laced a two-two pitch clear over the right-field fence. The freshmen were ahead 4-0 with none down. Del Bennett called time and headed for the mound.

Jim Collins was in his favorite seat, surrounded as always by the most rabid fans in the park. Collins had established himself as a real authority with this crowd, especially after the Wednesday onslaught the new kids had made on the varsity pitchers.

"Here we go again!" Collins yelled. "They're going to have to move the fences back for this group!"

"It's only the first inning, Jim," someone reminded him.

"Pretty good start!" Collins retorted. "Guess those steaks I fed the kids last night hit the spot. I had everybody there but Hilton and Smith," he added proudly.

Chip was sitting in the dugout. In the locker room, just before the game, Rockwell had designated Chip the starter for the final game. "If it's necessary, guys," Rockwell had said. "Personally, I think we'll sew it up this afternoon. Dean, you start. Nickels, you catch—"

Lefty Byrnes and Terrell Sparks were leaning on the railing of the freshman bullpen, watching the game. Silent Joe Maxim and Soapy were playing catch, leisurely throwing the ball back and forth, pausing from time to time to watch the developments in the game.

Soapy was strangely quiet. He scarcely opened his mouth, which was very, very unusual for Soapy. Yes, Soapy was deep in thought, planning something—a psychological campaign.

"They're powdering the ball," Sparks exulted. "We've got Bennett worried. He's trying to save Rickard for tomorrow. Hah! He shoulda used him today. What's that they say about there being no tomorrow? *Carpe diem.* Seize the day!"

"If our guys keep on like this, there won't be a tomorrow," Byrnes said lightly. "I'm hoping for that! Rockwell's got Hilton set for the feature spot tomorrow again. And I'd sure like to see that plan get spoiled!"

Sparks turned his head to study Byrnes. "You don't like Hilton, do you," he commented.

"Like him! You crazy? How could anyone like that swelled-headed grandstander?"

"I think you've got him wrong," Sparks protested. "I never met the guy until we started spring practice, but I watched him play football and basketball. He's got it! Seems like a pretty nice guy, too. One thing I know, he's one sweet ballplayer!"

"You're entitled to your own opinion, even if it is wrong," Byrnes said sullenly. "Anyone can star when the coach picks the spots."

"Well, there won't be any spots if he starts tomorrow. He'll be on his own all the way."

"On his own is right," Byrnes said cryptically.

The huddle on the mound disintegrated, leaving Harris to continue. Bennett had evidently decided to stay with the tall lefty. But there was activity in the varsity bullpen. Jeff "Slim" Burton and Ned Diston were throwing fast, warming up in a hurry. Hex Rickard, like Chip, was watching the game from the dugout. Bennett had notified the press and everyone else that Rickard would be the starting pitcher for the third game. And with that, Del had left no doubt in the minds of his listeners that he believed there would be a third game.

Belter Burke didn't get all the wood on the ball, but he drove George Reed, out in center field, all the way back to the fence for the catch. Durley hit sharply to the shortstop and was out by the proverbial whisker when Russ Merton made a perfect peg to first. Murph Gillen met one right on the nose, driving a lofty fly to left field, but Bill Bentley went back to pull it in for the third out. Lenny Harris had survived, but the freshmen had a big four-run lead.

The varsity led off with Russ Merton, and the little shortstop worked Dean for a walk. Tubby Ryder singled, and Bill Bentley, the power-hitting left fielder, pulled a shocker by laying a bunt to the left of the mound. Diz Dean made the try at third, but he had been caught by surprise, and Merton beat the throw with ease.

That loaded the bases and brought up George Reed, the varsity cleanup hitter. Reed swaggered up to the plate, big and powerful and confident. He pulled his bat through in a full practice swing, the rippling muscles of his bare forearms bulging with power. Reed seemed all set for a full swing.

Dean was cautious, got behind at two balls and no strikes, and thoughtlessly laid one down the middle. Then everyone except Del Bennett and Reed and the runners got a shock. Reed bunted! Merton was away with the pitch, and Dean, caught in the middle, waited too long to make a decision and ended up with the ball in his hand, never making a throw to any base.

FENCE BUSTERS

In the freshman bullpen, Flash Sparks began to burn pitches in to Soapy as he belatedly tried to get warmed up. Reggie Harris, the upperclassmen's towering first sacker, powdered the first pitch and drove the ball, straight as one of Tiger Woods's tee shots, up and out and over the 440-foot right-center fence. That cleared the bases and put the varsity out in front 5-4 and sent Diz Dean to the showers.

"Here we go," Byrnes said bitterly as Sparks started for the mound. "Setting the stage for the glamour boy!"

Sparks wasn't ready and walked Carter. But he got a break when Minson drove a hard grounder between shortstop and second. It looked as if the ball was in there for a hit, but Speed Morris came streaking across from deep short to scoop up the ball and relay it with an underhand toss to Crowell. Ozzie made a perfect pivot and throw to Cohen for the double play. Mitch Wilder popped up to Nickels for the third out, and the freshmen came trotting in, just one run behind. They were confident and cocky and eager for their turn and an opportunity to pulverize the ball.

Darrin Nickels, looking big and as solid as a rock, sauntered up to the plate, smiling and confident. Darrin looked at a ball and a strike and then clocked the next pitch with the fat of his bat. The ball took off in a slow-rising flight that carried it far over Bentley's head in left field and over the fence, vanishing somewhere in the forest of legs on the lacrosse field.

The fans cheered the burly catcher all around the base path, and Nickels came in smiling, doffing his cap as he crossed the plate. That evened it up at 5-5.

Rico Williams, the designated hitter, went down swinging. Crowell chopped a soft Texas leaguer over third base—a line drive that lofted over the infielder's head, then dropped gently to the grass in front of the left fielder. Morris slashed a hard ground ball between first and second, but Tubby Ryder made a sensational stop, knocking the ball down and then throwing to Merton for the force at second. It was two away. Bob Emery, eager and trying too hard, wouldn't look the pitches over and golfed a low inside one to Bentley for an easy third out.

The game rolled on much like Wednesday's game. But there was a difference in the methods used to get the runs. The freshmen were slugging away on their own whenever they were ahead of the pitcher. Rockwell was taking full advantage of the supreme confidence of his kids, playing the only cards at his disposal.

Del Bennett was using "hit" and "take" signs, the hit and run, the steal, the delayed double steal when men were on first and third, the double steal, the squeeze, and every strategy in the book. And, for all it was worth, he was directing the bunting game at the first-year pitchers.

Both coaches were right. Rockwell's team just wasn't capable of competing with the upperclassmen where inside baseball was concerned, but they were better hitters. Bennett had the better pitching, but his veterans couldn't compete with Rockwell's sluggers at the plate. It all added up to the kind of game fans love; they got a kick out of the hitting of the players and enjoyed a hundred opportunities to second-guess Bennett.

Sparks was getting a lot of on-the-job training fielding his position. Bennett's bunting game kept him busy. Too busy! Flash was having all kinds of trouble. So was Andre Durley! Bennett was using the bunt as a hit-and-run play, sending the runner on first down on the second or third pitch. Biggie, Sparks, and Durley would come dashing in to play the ball, and the hitter would lay it down the third-base line.

The second baseman, Ozzie Crowell, frequently got confused and tried to cover the steal. That left first open, and Durley had nowhere to throw the ball. He usually froze where he fielded the ball. Then the runner would go on to third. It was pretty to watch but hard to take.

Bennett was working another old strategy. With first and second occupied and none away, a varsity hitter would fake a bunt to see how Andre was going to react. If Durley showed he was going to field the ball, Bennett would put on a double steal, and the hitter would fake the bunt.

When Durley dashed in to field the bunt and found there was no play, he would try to get back to the bag to cover the base and, more often than not, he was in no position to take Nickels's throw. Morris tried to help Durley, but that meant leaving his position too soon, and Bennett's place hitters promptly lined one through the hole. Occasionally, a varsity hitter would push one past the charging Durley, and then Morris was in trouble.

It was a busy afternoon for Rockwell's pitchers and infielders. In the eighth, with the bases loaded and no one down, Rockwell sent Flash Sparks to the showers. No one would ever have known Rockwell had debated his next move for a long time. It was not apparent in his decisive motion for Byrnes. Yet the veteran coach was wondering if it was not giving the ill-tempered boy too much of a challenge. One thing was sure. A change had to be made if the game was to be won.

Rockwell had worked with boys all his life. He knew there came a time in the development of an athlete when the slack in the rope had to be tightened if the player was to develop into a real ballplayer. He figured the time had now come for Lefty Byrnes.

When Rockwell called, Byrnes put on an act. He was apparently surprised. He held up the game while he hurriedly threw a few extra pitches to Soapy before heading for the mound. And on the way he stopped to fix his shoelaces, picked up a blade of grass, and kept tossing his glove restlessly from hand to hand as he slowly advanced. Every action evidenced his displeasure.

Most of the fans remembered Byrnes's previous display of temper and were watching his approach with various thoughts. Many had written off his poor sportsmanship on Wednesday as the usual idiosyncrasy attributed to a left-hander. Others were openly disgusted with the pitcher. All were interested in observing his reaction to the present situation.

Jim Collins was typically optimistic. "Things will be a little different now," he ventured. "This big kid has the makings of one of the best in the game!"

"He didn't do a very good fielding job Wednesday," someone barked sarcastically.

"What's one error this early in the season!" Collins retorted.

"It doesn't mean a thing unless it gets to be a habit," a shrill voice observed.

"Since when is being temperamental a habit?"

"Temperament or temper?" the first fan demanded.

"I always thought a guy had to prove himself before he could afford to be temperamental," a third added.

"Some kids have to learn things the hard way," Collins said, quieting most of his personal badgerers. "It wouldn't hurt to remember he's just a kid."

It was too bad all the fans couldn't have heard Collins's last remark. They might have refrained from voicing their disapproval and restrained the chorus of boos that greeted Byrnes's arrival at the rubber.

Rockwell greeted Byrnes nonchalantly. In fact, he was smiling and appeared completely relaxed. "Don't worry about it, kid. Just blaze that fast one of yours in there a little on the high side and see what happens."

Byrnes didn't look at Rockwell. He waited with his eyes fixed on the pitching plate until Rockwell turned away. Then he sniffed contemptuously and shrugged his shoulders.

"C'mon, Lefty," Nickels said understandingly. "Show him up! Make him like it!"

"What's the use! This guy won't give anyone but Hilton a break!"

"Forget Hilton! Forget Rockwell too! Remember, you're in charge. This game is yours. C'mon, let's win this one! We're out in front by two runs! The weak end of the stick is up. Minson can't hit a curve, and Wilder's a sucker for anything inside. Burton doesn't even take the bat off his shoulder. C'mon, Lefty. This is your chance!"

In all justice to Byrnes, it should be said that he tried. But he hadn't brought himself up to the right emotional pitch. That was understandable too. Byrnes had always been a starting pitcher, a star who had been able to meet his competition with absolute confidence. But he was up against a very solid college ball club—a veteran team coached by a former major-leaguer. This was quite different from high school competition. The varsity was riding on a surge that had loaded the bases. There was no one down, and the upperclassmen were determined to get those ducks off the pond.

Minson was long past due. He was bursting with desire to dent the ball. But Bennett killed that ambition and called for the squeeze. Minnie responded beautifully and pushed one between Durley and Byrnes for his first hit of the game. Reed scored, and all hands were safe. Byrnes tried hard to reach the ball but couldn't quite make it. Morris came in fast and fielded the ball, but his throw to first was late. The varsity was now one run behind with no one away.

Standing behind the rubber, Byrnes appeared calm. But he was seething inside. He turned to look angrily at Morris and then faced Mitch "Widow" Wilder.

Widow was a picture of determination. He waited Lefty out until he got the pitch he wanted. It was a two-two fastball, letter-high, and Wilder pulverized the pitch for his first real blow of the series. The ball cleared the right-field fence by twenty feet, and the varsity was three runs ahead.

Byrnes got Burton on called strikes. Then he fanned Merton with a first-pitch called strike that split the plate, a fastball around the wrists that Merton went for too late, and a sharp breaking curve that ducked under Russ's bat on the outside corner. Ryder hit the ball high in the air over the box, and Biggie waved Byrnes away, making the catch for the third out.

Rockwell, waiting in front of the bat rack, attempted to pat Byrnes on the back. But the dejected hurler swerved aside and ducked under the protecting roof of the dugout.

"We'll get 'em back, Lefty," Nickels said soothingly.

"Don't worry about it," Morris said. "We'll hit!"

"That's for sure," Cohen added. "We'll get you some runs!"

Del Bennett crossed them up. Bennett sent Ned Diston, his number two-pitcher, in for the kill, and the fastball pitcher set the freshmen down in order. The varsity players didn't need the last turn at bat. They won the game 15-12 and evened the series at one game apiece.

Chip had suffered along with Byrnes during that hectic base-loaded inning and followed his teammates

FENCE BUSTERS

slowly up the hill to the field house. Most of the team had been eager to get away from the field and headed for the showers with disgruntled hearts. At the gate leading to the field house, Chip passed Byrnes and Nickels. He felt uncomfortable but couldn't resist expressing his sympathy.

"Tough breaks, Lefty," he said. "We'll get 'em tomorrow."

Byrnes's face flushed with rage. "Naturally," he said viciously. "Rockwell's wonder boy is pitching tomorrow!"

CHAPTER 7

Pitchers' Duel

SOAPY SMITH was a good student. The prankster was a good listener and possessed a wonderful capacity for absorbing information. He drank in every word in class and was able to retain the essential part of each lecture. Psychology 102 was his chief delight, and Professor Edna Smith was his favorite member of the faculty.

Soapy had cooperated in a number of Dr. Smith's psychology experiments, including participation as a hypnosis subject. Soapy liked the course, and not even Chip, his closest friend, knew he was seriously considering psychology as a major, in anticipation of a teaching career.

For the first time since fall semester exams, Soapy showed up behind Grayson's counter with a textbook. Fireball was shocked and kept asking Soapy if he was feeling all right. He was deeply solicitous, but Soapy ignored him and snatched every opportunity to concentrate feverishly on the text.

Most of the customers attributed Soapy's subdued spirits to the loss of the game. But they were entirely wrong. He was concentrating on a psychological angle, which would have delighted Dr. Smith. His unusually studious mood resulted in much inconvenience to his ice-cream customers, who liked Soapy but were a bit fed up with the "new dipper" line.

Chip noticed Soapy's preoccupation when they were on their way home but let it pass. He had a few things on his own mind. First and foremost was his mom in Valley Falls. Mary Hilton had returned to work after her operation to remove a cancerous tumor. She was feeling better than she had in a long time and had started swimming again. She'd have to return to Dr. Nader, her surgeon, every three months, but things were definitely looking positive.

His next concern was tomorrow's championship game. Long after he and Soapy had turned in, Chip was thinking about the varsity hitters and their weaknesses. He tossed and turned all night, living through a nightmarish dream in which he was pitching in his underwear and couldn't get the varsity out in the very first inning of the game.

Soapy was first up the next morning. He rushed to the window and anxiously surveyed the perfect sky. That was important news. "Hey, Chipper! Wake up! Sunshine! Gobs of it! Pitcher's delight! Hey, that's a good name for a sundae! Have to remember that! C'mon, let's get going! There's gonna be a million fans out there this afternoon," he chattered.

Soapy's estimate was slightly exaggerated, but there was a capacity crowd at two o'clock when the varsity trotted out on the field, hoping to carry on where it had left off the previous afternoon. Not that Soapy was any longer interested in spectators. No, Soapy had only one objective and that centered on Chip Hilton. During the warm-up in front of the grandstand, Soapy kept chattering away; he was setting his friend up for the big test. Chip hadn't been paying too much attention to Soapy, but the redhead's persistence eventually got his attention.

"I've never seen you faster, Chip," Soapy said, shaking his head. "Man, look at my hand! You're really burning it in today! And that was only warming up. Wish I had a steak—"

Chip grinned disarmingly, "You hungry already?"

"C'mon, Chip," Soapy protested. "You know what I mean. To put on my hand to keep the swelling down."

"I know, Soapy. Anyway, you're right. I never felt better."

Soapy looked at Chip suspiciously. Chip never bragged, and the statement chilled Soapy. But only for a second.

"Hope none of those guys get in the way of one of your hard ones," Soapy continued worriedly. "Boy, they better be wearing extra thick helmets! Think I ought to tell Bennett?"

"Oh, I don't think so. He probably knows what he's doing."

The umpire's "Play ball!" sent them into the dugout then and temporarily stopped their discussion—but not for long. Soapy went right back to work as soon as they were seated.

Hex Rickard looked extremely fast to Chip. The tall lefty's fastball seemed to have a hop on it, and Widow Wilder was making sure the pitches cracked like a ball meeting the fat of the bat as he caught them.

In fact, Chip thought the whole varsity looked unusually sharp. The ball went flying around the horn and across the diamond and back again without a slip. The fast, hard throws and their accuracy drew enthusiastic applause from the fans.

FENCE BUSTERS

Ozzie Crowell led off, batting from the right-hand side of the plate. Ozzie tried to work Rickard for a walk. It was pointless. Hex wasted nothing. He kept bearing down from the first pitch. He dropped his throws down around the stocky second baseman's knees and forced Ozzie to bounce a one-and-two pitch back to the mound. It was an easy out and a bad start. Crowell was tough up there, an ideal leadoff man, and so far in the series he had set the pace.

Morris had always been weak against any sort of a curve, and it was evident that the Widow and Hex knew that. Rickard's formula was simple. He drove Speed back from the plate and fed him a sharp curve. Then he drove him back again with an inside pitch and came back with a twisting curve that looked like a slow, off-speed pitch. Speed snapped at the bait but never touched the ball.

Bob Emery liked the fast ones, either high or low. The tall, wiry center fielder stood in the extreme back of the batter's box and made a pitcher work. Rickard worked Bob with the teasers: the curve, the sweeping curve, the screwball, and a knuckler that seemed to come out of nowhere across the plate. Emery, off balance, slugged away, but the best he could do was a short, lazy fly to right, which Lee Carter gobbled up for the third out.

The fans gave Rickard a good hand, but when Chip walked out to the mound, they nearly tore down the stands. Cheering, stomping their feet, and applauding, they told Chip exactly how they felt about his play during the series. They hadn't forgotten that first game!

Jim Collins, on his feet and yelling his head off, nearly kicked a hole in the back of the seat in front of him. The occupant was forced to stand up for self-protection. He turned around, exasperation written all over his face.

"Are you crazy, Jim?" the angry man shouted, trying to make himself heard above the crowd's roar.

Collins nodded happily. "And how!" he shouted back. "He sure is good! The best hurler in the country! And he powders the ball too!" He turned back to look at the diamond. "Y-e-a-a-a-h!"

Gee-Gee Gray, sitting in the announcer's booth, was yakking away, the words spilling rapidly from his mouth. Gee-Gee was in his element broadcasting the game he loved.

"And here comes the kid now! Coming out for the warm-up throws. It's a tough spot for a kid. Listen to the crowd! The fans like this young man!

"This is a crucial game. By the way, some of you may be wondering why the varsity has been the home team and has had their hits last in the series. Well, it seems it's one of State's sports traditions—the team that wins the series the preceding year becomes the home team the following year. Rather than hosting another varsity collegiate team as they have each preceding year, State decided to play the freshman team. Since the freshman team is new this year with State's new pilot athletic program, they're the visiting team—at least this year.

"Right now, your old Gee-Gee would like to go out on a limb. Yes, I want to predict that next year's new kids will bat last in the preseason series. Why? That's easy! Because one of the greatest young pitchers I've ever seen has finished his warm-up pitches and is set to go to work. And I expect Coach Henry Rockwell will have Hilton somewhere in the lineup as a hitter too. The freshman catcher, Robert 'Soapy' Smith, has pegged the ball down to second base, and I mean pegged. Smith can really throw to the bases. Hilton's got the ball now, and here comes the best leadoff guy in college baseball today: Russ Merton."

FENCE BUSTERS

Lefty Byrnes and Flash Sparks had been loosening up and throwing the ball to Nickels in the bullpen. When the freshmen took the field and Chip headed for the mound, the burst of applause, echoing again and again, carried clear to the end of the field. Byrnes turned to watch and was joined by Sparks and Nickels.

Flash glanced at Byrnes when the cheers died down, noting the grim expression clouding the lefty's face. There was a mischievous gleam in Sparks's eyes. "You see the *Herald* this morning?"

Byrnes shook his head, and Sparks continued. "Bill Bell said Hilton was the best all-around freshman athlete he'd seen in twenty years—maybe in the history of the school."

Byrnes grunted disdainfully. "Bill Bell! What's that old goat know about sports?"

"He's the sports editor!"

"So what! Anyone who's in with the owner of a paper can be the sports editor."

"I don't know about that! Anyway, Bell's been with the *Herald* for nearly thirty years."

"What's that got to do with it?"

"Why, even a monkey would learn something about sports after writing about them for thirty years. Bell said he wouldn't be surprised if Hilton shut out the varsity. He said lots of pitchers are ahead of the hitters this early in the season and that Hilton isn't just any pitcher."

Byrnes glanced significantly at Nickels. "He might have a surprise coming before the season's over. Besides, how does Bell account for the score of the first game if pitchers are ahead of the hitters?"

"Yeah," Nickels added. "Lots of flowers bloom only in the spring."

Sparks glanced at the roommates curiously but said nothing. That didn't mean he wasn't thinking. Flash

PITCHERS' DUEL

Sparks was an easygoing person and an outstanding pitcher in his own right, but Flash believed in giving credit where credit was due, and he agreed with Bill Bell. Flash recognized Chip's ability and was glad to have him as a teammate even though they were rivals for a starting berth. Sparks couldn't understand why Byrnes and Nickels were so antagonistic. After an awkward silence, he shrugged his shoulders and concentrated on the action.

Russ Merton was a cocky little guy. He stood shorter than five-seven, and when he crouched at the plate, the strike zone all but vanished. But that wasn't all. Merton crowded forward and kept his head bobbing and weaving over the plate.

Chip was worried about Merton's head and threw everything overhanded, keeping his pitches low. He fed Russ a fastball, a screwball, and a curve. The two dueled away until it was the full count. Then Chip came in with a low fastball, and Russ hit the ball hard. But it was on the ground, a high hopper that Andre Durley took chest-high and clotheslined across to Cohen. Merton was out by thirty feet.

Tubby Ryder looked like Durley. If anything, he was shorter and stockier than Andre. The husky, hot corner guardian stood about five-six and had an eagle eye. A pitcher had to put the ball right down the middle to tempt Tubby. Chip put it down the middle for the "take" pitch and then tried a low outside curve, which Tubby watched impassively, ignoring the pitch completely. Chip figured Ryder would go for the one and one and blazed it down with all the speed at his command. Tubby swung hard but topped the hard-breaking ball toward second. Ozzie Crowell took the streaker and casually tossed the ball to Cohen for out number two.

FENCE BUSTERS

That brought up Bill Bentley, and Soapy called time. Advancing to the mound, Soapy practically rubbed noses with Chip while he talked. Ostensibly, Bentley was the subject of the discussion. Actually, Soapy was complaining about his hand.

"Man, Chip, I've got to do something about this glove. I never knew you could throw so hard. Merton and Ryder hit the ball because they couldn't get the bat out of the way. You be careful where you're throwing, 'cause if you hit anyone today, you'll break an arm or something. I'm gonna ask for a new ball. This one's got a blem—a blem—a spot on it, and I can hardly see it."

Chip smiled. "I know, Soapy, I know. I never threw so hard in my life. My arm feels like a rubber band. I wonder what's come over me. I've never felt like this before."

Soapy was grinning widely as he hustled back to the plate. He was mentally patting himself on the back. "It's working," he muttered gleefully. "It's working!"

"What's that?" the umpire demanded, glaring suspiciously at Soapy. "You talking to me?"

"What's that?" Soapy echoed. "Oh, no, sir! I was just talking to myself, sir. Sir, can we have a new ball? I can't see the one we're using."

"Now look here," the umpire thundered. "You just cut out that funny stuff and play ball. Understand?"

Soapy nodded. "Yes, sir," he said. But he didn't mean it. He wasn't cutting out anything! Not while Chip was cooperating so beautifully! He only hoped Dr. Smith was in the stands.

Bentley, batting left-handed, didn't have any trouble seeing the ball. He hit the first pitch! It was an inside pitch that the left fielder caught high on the handle and looped over third. It looked as if the ball might drop in for a hit, but Morris showed the fans how he got his

PITCHERS' DUEL

nickname by darting swiftly to his right and making an almost impossible running backhand catch. Speed stabbed at the looper just before it hit the ground and tumbled head over heels. But he held the ball! Chip breathed a sigh and trotted across the baseline to pat the speedster on the back and walk with him to the dugout. Speed got a big hand.

It was that kind of ball game all the way. The freshmen hit the ball every inning, but Rickard's stuff was breaking, and solid blows were few and far between. The underclassmen knicked him for three singles, but none produced a run. Chip had hurled perfect ball. He hadn't allowed a hit. Soapy was bursting with importance and joy. He could scarcely restrain the urge to tell someone, anyone, his secret.

The freshmen got men on base time after time, but they couldn't score. With a duck on the pond, they'd hit a terrific grounder that a varsity infielder would somehow manage to field. With no one on, someone would pound a ball to the outfield, but it would head straight for one of the varsity outfielders as if it had eyes.

Biggie Cohen hit one over the right-field fence in the sixth, inches to the right of the foul-line marker. In the seventh, Chip, batting right-handed against Rickard's darting fastball, hit a hard liner into left field. But Bill Bentley called on all of his tremendous speed to make a sensational over-the-shoulder catch.

Del Bennett tried his bunt game, but Chip chilled that strategy, covering the area in front of the plate like a blanket and throwing out every hitter who dared to lay one down.

So the game rocked along through the ninth and into the top of the tenth. Rickard struck Durley out with three fast ones. Then, for the first time, his control slipped, and he walked Gillen. Rockwell gambled then, called for time, and sent for Nickels to pinch hit for Soapy.

"Surprise, surprise," Byrnes sneered when Nickels started for the diamond. "About time the guy quit playing favorites. He must really want to win the game."

Rockwell wanted to win the game, all right. And he wasn't playing favorites or safe or anything but heads-up baseball. He had made up his mind to sacrifice Gillen to second and leave it up to Chip to win his own game. He stopped Nickels at the third-base coaching box and gave him his instructions, talking softly so he wouldn't be heard.

"Wait for a good one and lay it down. Rickard probably will figure you for the sacrifice or Gillen for the steal. He won't give you anything good, that's for sure. Look them over, and then, when he has to come in with a fat one, lay it down! OK, Darrin, it's up to you. Push Gillen along, and Chip will bring him in. He'll hit!"

Nickels turned away without a word and headed for the bat rack. "Hilton again," he growled. "Always Hilton! *He* can hit. Humph!"

CHAPTER 8

Serving Knuckleball Pitches

DARRIN NICKELS had a good eye. He was a consistent .300 hitter and hit the long ball. He worked Rickard for a two-and-no count and then stepped out of the box and eyed Rockwell in the coaching box at third base. Rockwell turned his back, indicating no change in the sign, and Nickels stepped back up to the plate.

Rickard delivered, and Nickels shocked Rockwell and every player in the dugout when he swung viciously at the pitch. It was a letter-high pitch, and Nickels cut under the ball, sending a high foul back to the screen. Widow Wilder flipped off his mask and scurried back to take the pop-up for out number two. Gillen was still anchored at first.

Rockwell rushed from the coaching box and met Nickels in front of the dugout. Rock was almost speechless. "What happened?" the flustered coach demanded. "How come?"

Nickels didn't answer but began strapping on his shin guards. Rockwell was puzzled. "What were you thinking about? You deliberately crossed up the play! Why?"

Nickels finished buckling the shin guards and straightened up. But he didn't meet Rockwell's eyes. He pulled the chest protector over his head and stood there without saying a word.

Rockwell drew a deep breath and glanced beyond Nickels to Chip, who was waiting in the on-deck circle. "All right," he said in resignation, gesturing Chip toward the plate, "you're on your own. Two away, remember."

Nickels ducked into the dugout, and Rockwell, still bewildered, hustled back to the coaching box.

Chip had a healthy respect for Rickard. The lanky southpaw worked the corners, avoided the middle of the plate, and studied every hitter. And Rickard had a healthy respect for Chip Hilton, especially his hitting ability. Hex hadn't forgotten Chip's game-winning home run off Diston, and, he remembered more recently, the fastball Chip had tagged in the seventh. Now Hex looked steadily at the varsity dugout, waiting for Del Bennett to decide whether he should issue Chip an intentional pass or work on him. Bennett spread his hands, palms up. That left it up to Rickard, and he decided to pitch. "The kid has to be tired," Hex told himself. "I'll strike him out!"

Chip took the first pitch for a called strike. He watched a curve go by when it broke inches inside for a ball. And he got behind when he fouled another inside curve off the handle. Rickard decided to get it over with and came in with an overhand fastball between the belt and knees. Chip belted it, golfing it in a high, whirling bender that headed out toward right center and curved clear to the right-field fence, just inches inside the foul line.

Every fan in the park was on his feet, shifting his eyes between Lee Carter chasing the ball in the right corner of the field and Murph Gillen racing around the bases. Rockwell, waving Gillen home, was a whirling turnstile in the coaching box.

The throw and Gillen and Wilder all converged at the plate, but Murph slid under and across before Widow Wilder tagged him—the freshmen had their first run. Chip pulled up at third.

Ozzie Crowell hit the first pitch hard, but it was a straightaway fly ball which George Reed pulled in for the third out. It didn't seem too important with that big number 1 standing out as prominently as a black eye among all the zeros on the scoreboard.

Soapy stopped Nickels when his replacement started for the plate. "Chip's as smooth as silk, Darrin," he said cordially. "He'll put it right where you want it."

"Yeah, right!" Nickels said shortly.

The surly receiver made no attempt to check the signs with Chip. He simply squatted behind the plate and gave the sign for a fastball. Chip shook it off. He had Lee Carter figured. Carter batted from the right side of the plate and liked fastballs. Nickels then called for a curve, and Chip slipped a called strike across on the inside.

Then Chip got a big surprise. Nickels burned the ball back to the mound on Chip's right side. The vicious throw was unexpected, and Chip went for the ball without thinking, partly catching it with his throwing hand. The impact on his bare hand resulted in a sharp numbing sensation that was almost unbearable. But Chip controlled his impulse to give in to the pain and walked slowly behind the mound.

"That won't happen again, mister," Chip breathed. Standing there with his hands behind his back, he clenched and unclenched his fist in an attempt to get some feeling into his fingers. But when he tried to grip the ball, his fingers would not respond. "Time, ump," he called. "Time!"

Henry Rockwell had keen, black eyes. And he used them. Rock didn't miss much on a baseball field. He had seen the unnecessarily hard return Nickels made and the fleeting expression of pain on Chip's face when he caught the ball. And he had been relieved when Chip gave no indication of sustaining an injury. Now he was alarmed. Chip wouldn't call time unless he was badly hurt. Rockwell was out on the field almost as soon as the umpire raised his hands to stop play. Soapy was right behind him.

Chip clamped his glove under his left arm and looked at his throwing hand for the first time. "No wonder," he muttered. "No wonder."

The middle finger was bent almost all the way back. It was incongruously out of place. And the pain was intense. Before he could do anything about it, he was surrounded.

"Oh, no," Biggie said. "Here's trouble."

"Not much," Chip said. "Here, just pull it back in place."

Biggie recoiled. "Not me!"

"Nor anyone else!" Rockwell interrupted. "We'll let the trainer take care of that!"

"It's all right, Coach," Chip remonstrated. "It's only out of place."

The varsity dugout had stilled and the fans had quieted, except for a chorus of questions, answers, and opinions. Del Bennett was out on the field now, accompanied by the team physician, Dr. Mike Terring. Immediately, Terring took charge.

"Hold still, Chip," he said. "This will only take a second."

There was a little snap, and Chip felt a quick spasm of pain and then relief. "Wow, that feels better," he said. "I'll be all right now."

Henry Rockwell was watching anxiously. "How about it, Doc?" he asked apprehensively. "Can he go on?"

Terring made no reply. He was exploring the injury with practiced hands, gently pressing the finger with his thumb, probing for a fracture.

Rockwell was undecided. Under ordinary circumstances he would have unhesitatingly sent Chip to the dugout. But this was different. Rock had several reasons for his desire to let Chip finish this game.

Soapy was concentrating. His lips moved soundlessly as he called on his newly found power for help. Soapy had his own particular reason for wanting Chip to carry on.

"Try to bend the finger, Chip," Terring suggested.

Chip tried, but it was no go. The finger had puffed up now and was as stiff as a board. "I can't move it much, Doc," Chip said quietly. "But I don't think it will mean much when I throw."

Terring smiled. "Gonna use knucklers exclusively?"

Chip nodded, "I might!"

"All right, Hank," Terring said. "I'll tape it, and you can leave him in the game if you wish. It won't hurt the finger if he can throw."

"I can throw!" Chip said grimly.

"By the way," Terring added, "report to me right after you shower. I want to take an X-ray." He turned to Rockwell. "Everything feels OK, Hank, but I want to be sure."

"OK, Chipper," Rockwell agreed. "Give it a try."

Nickels was standing on the fringe of the group, and Biggie Cohen edged around until he was close beside the burly receiver. "Listen, Nickels," Biggie said gently, "you watch how you throw that ball back to the pitcher. Understand? You understand what I'm talking about?"

Nickels nodded and turned away, but his troubles weren't over. Rockwell took him by the arm and walked him back to the plate. Keeping a firm grip on the big catcher's arm, Rockwell spoke rapidly and sternly. "That was a dirty move, Nickels. Stay in the game, but it's your last chance. Don't ever cross me up again on the signs, and you make sure you throw that ball back to the pitcher the way it's supposed to be thrown back—on the *glove-hand* side."

The fans knew what had happened, and they gave Chip a tremendous round of applause when it was apparent that he was going to continue. The varsity players joined in that hand too.

With the count on Carter at no balls and one strike, Nickels squatted and gave the sign for a fastball. Chip shook that off, not too sure he could throw the ball at all, much less a fastball. They settled on a curve, and Chip breathed a little prayer as he delivered the ball. Miraculously, it headed for the plate, but there was nothing on the pitch. Carter stepped into it as though it were a batting-practice throw.

There was a sharp crack, and the ball took off like a flash of light down the left-field foul line. It was fair, and Belter Burke got on his horse and tore toward the fence without looking back. Belter never broke stride and never turned his head until the precise instant the ball arrived. Then he threw up his glove hand and made the catch over his shoulder, running at full speed. The fans gave the big outfielder a terrific hand of applause.

Chip had been massaging his finger while the ball was in the air, and he was glad Speed took the throw from Burke and trotted in with the ball.

"Bear down, Chipper," Speed pleaded. "Only two to go!"

Minnie Minson had big hands, strong arms, and powerful shoulders. And he liked a long bat. Chip remembered precisely what he had thrown to the husky third baseman Wednesday, but he was afraid to try the screwball—afraid it might get away. But the curve hadn't even been a good excuse. Then he remembered Terring's remark. Well, he'd try it! He'd feed them knucklers.

Minson was waiting for the next batting-practicelike toss and let the first one go by for a called strike. Then Chip got another surprise. Nickels walked out in front of the plate and almost startled Chip by chortling, "Atta baby, big boy! Throw it in here!" Then Darrin tossed the ball back on Chip's glove side and walked slowly back to his position. He took a long time getting set. It was evident to everyone that Nickels was using up all the time he could.

Chip welcomed the delay. His fingers were feeling better all the time. He kept shaking off the signs until Nickels got around to the knuckleball again. Minson swung at the wobbly ball with all his might and missed. But the effort brought a mighty "Ah" from the stands.

Nickels was wise now. He started the signs with the knuckler, and Chip nodded. Minnie was dug in and hoping for a fastball. Chip faked it well. The ball left his hand and shot up, out, and down just as it had on Wednesday. And just as before, Minson stopped his swing and then tried to murder the ball. He missed it by a mile. That made it two outs, and the freshmen were one out away from a great victory.

Jim Collins was praising Chip to the skies. "Imagine that kid," he was yelling to everyone within hearing distance. "Imagine him pitching with a busted hand? You guys see the stuff on that knuckler? You see how he can control it? I bet there haven't been five pitchers in this school's history who could control a knuckler like that."

Nickels burned the ball down to first after the strike-out, and while it went winging around the infield, Chip refreshed his memory on Wilder. Widow Wilder was a switch hitter, but he liked to bat right-handed. Maybe he could coax the knuckler low on the outside if Wilder hit from the third-base side of the plate.

Wilder took quite a while choosing a bat and then walked up to the right-handed side of the plate. Chip faked the fastball, but it was a wasted effort. Bennett had figured it out and knew now that Chip couldn't throw anything but the knuckler, and Wilder was looking for it. Chip let it go anyway, and Widow timed his swing perfectly. But he missed the ball!

The knuckler is an unpredictable pitch as the ball follows no prescribed course. One time it bobs left, the next time, right.

Wilder stepped angrily out of the box. Then, on a sudden hunch, he made a great show of moving around to the first-base side of the plate. Chip didn't mind. He came in again with the knuckler, and this time Wilder hit it with what most fans called a "loud foul." The ball floated up in the air along the first-base foul line and into the bleachers.

Nickels took the new ball from the umpire and sent it out to Chip. Once more Chip put all of his hopes, his back, his arm, and his wrist into the knuckleball. The ball flashed up and out and then darted down and bounced on the ground and across the plate, before careening off Nickels's shin guards. Wilder swung so hard he nearly fell, but he missed the ball. Widow was so perplexed that he forgot to run on the dropped third strike. And while Widow was standing there berating himself, oblivious to his teammates' pleas to run, Nickels retrieved the ball and tagged him out.

The freshmen had won the series. Chip Hilton had a thirteen-strikeout victory . . . and a *no-hitter!*

CHAPTER 9

"Watch This One, Rockwell!"

GRAYSON'S WAS packed! Every baseball fan in town and every freshman in school wanted to see Chip Hilton. Chip had kept himself busy and out of sight in the storeroom. But Mitzi Savrill, who always had an eye out for business, drew George Grayson's attention to the three-deep crowd standing in front of the counter. She subtly mentioned that Chip had pitched a no-hitter. That did it! Grayson chalked up another triumph for his petite genius, and in a few minutes Chip was behind the counter.

Chip's appearance created such a disturbance that even passersby couldn't restrain their curiosity. They crowded inside to add to the confusion. Soapy was doing a landslide business with Grayson's newest novelty, "Pitcher's Delight," but he took time out to lead a cheer for Chip as he served his creation to the returning blond.

At closing time, Chip got another tribute engineered by Mitzi and Mr. Grayson. While Chip was working at the counter, Mrs. Grayson was supervising preparations in the office for an informal staff party in the no-hitter's honor.

Chip was overwhelmed. He'd been mobbed by most of his teammates in the locker room after the game and tossed into the shower. Then tonight, he'd been on the receiving end of congratulations at the counter. And now he had to go through it all again. "Really," he protested, "I didn't do anything! Why, if Burke, Speed, Soapy, Biggie, and all the guys hadn't played such great defense, I'd probably be the losing pitcher."

Despite his protests, no one got the idea that Chip was displeased. Far from it! But he honestly felt his teammates weren't getting enough credit for the victory. He was glad when the party was over, and he was on his way home with Soapy.

Soapy was bubbling over. He just had to tell Chip the big secret. "Chipper," he said haltingly, "you know Dr. Smith's ideas about suggestion and thoughts and all that stuff?"

Chip grinned delightedly. "Yes, I know, Soapy."

"Well, I tried it today. I hope you don't mind. I was putting all that stuff in operation from the very beginning. Guess I sorta fibbed to you about my hand and everything, but I was determined you'd get a no-hitter. And, well, I guess the means justify the end, or whatever it is. And I hope you'll forget it."

"Sure, Soapy," Chip said seriously. "It's OK."

When Chip and Soapy walked up the front steps of Jeff and entered the hall, they got a shock. Every light on the first floor suddenly flashed on and a hundred voices yelled out with a cheer.

Chip never did learn how his dormmates had managed it, but Jeff threw a big midnight dorm party, and

Pete Randolph, the resident assistant, was right in the middle of it. Hot dogs, burgers, pizza, and Cokes covered every surface of the first-floor lounge.

Chip was exhausted when he finally escaped, but as he trudged up the stairs to the second floor, he could hear Soapy explaining the part sports psychology had played in victories such as today's shutout no-hitter.

Chip chuckled as he undressed. Soapy was a great guy, and he wouldn't hurt him for the world. Fireball Finley had told him the Jim Collins psychology story before he spilled it to Soapy. Chip grinned again. He'd have to check with Fireball to make sure Soapy didn't find out that he knew the Collins psychology story by heart.

Soapy was up early Sunday morning. The redhead was waiting for the newspapers' delivery and grabbed one of Jeff's sixty-odd papers before he dashed up the stairs two at a time. It didn't take him long to find the story. It was stretched across the top of the first page of the sports section.

"Chip! Wake up! Look at this!"

HILTON WINS OWN GAME AND CAMPUS CHAMPIONSHIP
Pitches No-Hitter, Wins 1-0

by Bill Bell

William "Chip" Hilton, freshman star hurler, won his own game yesterday afternoon at Alumni Field, 1-0.

With two down in the top of the tenth and Murph Gillen on first base, Hilton connected for a three-bagger that drove in the lone tally of the game.

"WATCH THIS ONE, ROCKWELL!"

It was a brilliant personal victory for the young hurler, who pitched through the last frame with an injured hand. Hilton struck out the last two batters who faced him to register thirteen strikeouts in ten innings.

Hector "Hex" Rickard pitched a steady game for the varsity and received fine support from his teammates, but he couldn't match the peerless pitching of Coach Rockwell's freshman phenom.

Hilton gets credit for both of his team's victories, and as a result of his performance in the campus championship series, he ranks as the number-one pitcher on campus. Young Hilton not only did a first-rate whitewash job of the varsity hitters, but he also hit brilliantly in the clutch, winning both games with timely blows.

"That's terrible," Chip groaned. "What will the rest of the team think? That reads as though I won the game all by myself."

"You did," Soapy said firmly. "Wait, there's more—"

"Please, Soapy. I don't want to hear it. Doesn't Bell say *anything* about the other guys?"

"Not much! Why should he?"

"Now you're being silly."

The longer the argument continued, the less ground Chip gained. He finally gave up, seeking refuge in his books.

Several other readers wouldn't have sided with Chip Hilton in anything, except for Chip's side of the argument with Soapy. Lefty Byrnes was angrily berating Bill Bell and Chip Hilton and Henry Rockwell. *And* his listeners agreed with everything he said. Darrin Nickels, Ellis Burke, and Murphy Gillen were good and irate.

"We might as well turn in our uniforms," Burke said bitterly.

"That's right," Murph Gillen agreed. "Why don't we?"

"I wouldn't give Rockwell and the glamour boy that much satisfaction," Byrnes said stubbornly. "There are other ways."

"What other ways?" Nickels asked.

"Just ways," Byrnes said evasively. "Stick around and you'll find out."

An athlete who enjoys sports fame is a magnet for all sorts of fans. Chip was in the limelight because of his baseball prowess, and there wasn't anything he could do about it. The phone rang all morning with calls from close and not so close friends and classmates who wanted to congratulate him. Right after lunch, Jim Collins showed up with Fireball Finley and practically abducted Chip and Soapy.

"You promised," Collins said. "Remember? Remember, you said you'd come out to the farm the first Sunday you had a chance. Well, this is the first Sunday! Bring your books."

Later, Chip was glad Jim Collins had taken them to the farm. The house and the barns were slightly run-down, but the meadows, pastures, and woodlands were leafing out with the beautiful greens of spring. It was gorgeous. The peaceful quiet of the country was a welcome change from Chip's busy college life, and the genuine friendliness of Jim Collins and Cindy was heartwarming. Chip was truly sorry when it was time to go home.

He got the hero treatment all day Monday from his classmates. After a while Chip gave up trying to be modest. He accepted the praise for what it was worth and tried to give as much credit as possible to his teammates.

"WATCH THIS ONE, ROCKWELL!"

He was relieved when he had finished with his last class and could head for Dr. Terring's office.

Terring was all smiles. "It's OK, Chip. No break. But you'll have to go easy on the throwing for a few days. I've already told Coach Rockwell. Now let me check that splint and give it some new tape. By the way, when you're hitting, grip the bat. Don't baby that finger. The more you use it, except for throwing, the quicker it will heal. All right?"

Chip could feel the tension as soon as he walked into the locker room. Nobody said anything, but the feeling was as expressive as words would have been. The usual clubhouse banter was missing; there were no wisecracks and not much talking of any kind. Biggie and Soapy tried to break through the barrier by praising Belter Burke's great catch and Gillen's base-running, but the two players' sullen response was without warmth.

Henry Rockwell sensed the trouble as soon as the players reported to the practice field. Rock knew the signs. He had met this problem innumerable times during his thirty years of coaching. His antidote was simple: "Bear down and keep them busy. Make them hustle for their jobs."

The wily coach went right to work, wasting no time on compliments. "Let's go! Infielders over here in two rows for a little pepper ball. Outfielders go to the sliding area. Pitchers and catchers loosen up over there in front of the bleachers. Hilton, you fall in with the outfielders."

Chip liked the way the coach handled the situation. He took his turn with the slides, protecting his finger, and put everything he had into the drill. Rockwell was thorough. He made a player come in on the left and the right with the hook slide, made him take off with both feet, diving headfirst for the bag, and made him work on getting back to a base.

FENCE BUSTERS

It was a tough workout. Ballplayers always gripe about the "tough" coach, who bears down, who makes them work hard. But that's the coach they respect and remember longest. Rockwell was remembered a long time by any player who worked under him. After half an hour, Rockwell ordered the infielders to the sliding pit and sent the outfielders to the diamond for some base-running and sign practice.

A scattering of spectators and fans began to show up about this time in the bleachers, and Jim Collins was among them. As usual, Collins called out a loud hello to every player in sight. Jim called them by their first names and was proud he was a personal friend of each of the young athletes. The big farmer had a way with kids; a lot of young people could have testified to that trait. Jim was a real friend.

Rockwell gave Collins a break that afternoon. He asked him to fungo flies to the outfielders while he handled the infield.

Chip liked to chase flies. What ballplayer didn't? And Dr. Terring's admonition to refrain from throwing with his injured right hand was no handicap. Chip could throw a long ball with his left hand.

"Here you go, Hilton," Collins called when it was Chip's turn. "Get on your horse!"

Collins lifted a long, high fly to Chip's right. Chip tore after it with flying legs, pulled it in with a backhand stab, pivoted, thrust the glove under his right arm, and threw the ball in with his left hand.

The ball came in on a line, and Collins nearly dropped the bat. "Did you see that?" he called to the fans in the bleachers. "Did you see that throw? *Left-handed!*"

Jim Collins wasn't the only one who was surprised. The pitchers heard Collins and turned to watch as Chip gathered in another high fly and pegged the ball back with his left hand.

"Show-off!" Byrnes sneered. "More grandstand stuff!"

"I don't think so," Sparks countered. "I think it's great. I wish I could do it! What's he do with the ball when he catches it?"

"Leaves it in the glove," Maxim explained.

Rod "Diz" Dean demonstrated. "Like this," he said. "He catches the ball in the glove with his left hand, shoves the glove with the ball still in it under his arm, pulls his hand out of the glove, and takes the ball out of the glove with his left hand, see? Then he throws the ball with his left hand. I used to play with a one-armed guy. He played the outfield for us. Boy, what a throw he could make!"

"I still say it's grandstand stuff," Byrnes griped. "What reason's Hilton got to throw left-handed?"

"Simple enough," Sparks argued. "He's got a bad right hand. Remember, he's a switch hitter; he bats from either side. Why shouldn't he throw left-handed if he has the ability? Maybe he's a natural lefty like you are."

"That's right," Joe Maxim added. "I was born a lefty, but my folks changed me to a righty. I wish they'd left me alone."

Rockwell broke up the conversation. "All right," he shouted. "Batting practice! Managers, roll that cage up behind the plate. Infielders do the chasing! Outfielders hit!

"Byrnes, you throw! Nickels and Smith, feed the balls. Let's go! On the double now! Hit three and lay one down and run it out!"

Byrnes didn't like it. Star hurlers frequently get the idea that pitching for batting practice is beneath their dignity. Some managers assign their pitchers to batting-practice pitching as a sort of punishment or to eliminate overconfidence in their abilities. Other managers feel the risk of injury to a member of the pitching staff, or to a regular player, is too great and prefer to use reserve members of the squad for the chore. But most good pitchers welcome the opportunity to loosen up, get the feel of the mound, develop form, and work on the finish of their delivery and fielding position.

Byrnes sullenly and slowly made his way out to the mound. And when he delivered the ball, the result was a halfhearted throw that was about as much value in developing timing and a hitting eye as being a spectator.

Rockwell, busying himself with the equipment, apparently was unaware of the temperamental southpaw's rebellious attitude. But Rock was still trying to build character. Perhaps reconstructing or repairing would have been more correct. Anyway, he was still trying to bring the unruly southpaw around, and the practice pitching was a part of the program.

Byrnes continued the indifferent throwing, and some of the hitters complained. "Come on, Lefty, throw it as though you meant it."

The plea went unheeded, and Rockwell decided to take a stand. "Put a little something on the ball, Byrnes," he called. "Those tosses are a waste of time." Byrnes mumbled something under his breath and then began recklessly blazing the ball toward the plate.

Chip was on deck, swinging a couple of extra bats, and stepped up to the third-base side of the plate when Murph Gillen laid down a bunt and sprinted to first.

Chip had good hitting form. His wide stance and high-poised bat indicated power, and each time he snapped his wrists at the end of the swing, the ball took off, scarcely rising higher than the pitch. But it carried clear and straight to the fence, and the crack of the bat against the ball brought a twist of satisfaction to Chip's lips. The blows brought a spatter of applause from the bleachers too.

That was the last straw as far as Byrnes was concerned. He frowned grimly as he turned for another ball. Sending pitches up for anyone was bad enough, but it was too much if Chip Hilton was concerned. Byrnes was almost beside himself now. "Waste of time, huh?" he muttered. "Well, watch this one, Rockwell!"

Chip knew Byrnes was angry, but there was nothing he could do about it. Right now he was concerned only with sharpening his hitting eye. He stepped across the plate to the first-base side for the bunt. He pulled his batting helmet down over his right eye and focused on the delivery. Chip never had a chance to lay that one down. Byrnes stepped toward first and blazed a sidearm throw straight for Chip's head.

"Look out!" Soapy shouted, his voice shrill with alarm. "Look *out!*"

The warning came too late. Chip ducked frantically, dropping the bat and throwing his right arm up in protection. But fast as he was, the ball was faster. It smacked against his elbow, the crack of the ball against flesh and bone ringing out above the warning shout. There was a shocked silence, and then the players ran to Chip's side. Biggie Cohen and Soapy Smith got there first. "You all right?" they chorused. "You all right, Chip?"

Chip answered with his eyes. He gripped his right elbow with his left hand, scarcely able to stand the agonizing pain that paralyzed his arm. He tried to bend the elbow, but the pain was too much. "Oh, man, it hurts," he managed.

CHAPTER 10

Biggie Speaks His Mind

DR. TERRING couldn't believe his eyes. "Oh, no!" he cried. "Not you again! This is too much! Help him off with that shirt. Easy. Sit up here on the table. Now what happened?"

"Hit by a wild pitch," Chip explained. "I couldn't get out of the way fast enough."

"Wild pitch? No way!" Soapy exploded. "Byrnes tried to *bean* him!"

Concern flooded Terring's face. "You sure of that?" he asked in a shocked voice.

Soapy nodded emphatically. "I know it!"

"He didn't mean to hit me, Soapy," Chip said, looking to Biggie for support. But Biggie, siding with Soapy, nodded affirmatively.

"Yes, he did!" Soapy insisted. "Biggie heard him and so did I! He said, 'All right, Rockwell, watch this.' Or something like that. Right, Biggie?"

"That's right!" Biggie said shortly.

"That doesn't mean he deliberately tried to hit me with the ball," Chip said. "He could have meant a lot of things. He could have meant he was going to strike me out or throw some real hard stuff or almost anything."

"He'll get some hard stuff," Soapy threatened. "The first chance—"

Chip interrupted him. "No, he won't, Soapy. Forget it! Besides, this is my problem."

"Some problem!" Cohen observed bitterly.

Dr. Terring gently probed and pressed away at Chip's elbow. "I don't think there's anything broken, Chip," he said, straightening up and rubbing his chin reflectively. "But we'll soon know. We'll take an X-ray."

Terring turned to Biggie and Soapy, "You guys can go on back to practice if you want to. This is going to take about an hour."

"We'd rather wait if you don't mind," Biggie said quietly.

Soapy nodded. "Practice is about over, Doc."

A little later, Red Schwartz, Speed Morris, Terrell Sparks, Ozzie Crowell, Andre Durley, and Rod Dean crowded into the room.

"Is it bad?" Speed asked.

Terring appeared just then and answered the question. "It doesn't look too bad," he said, fastening the negative to the glass reflector. "Not bad at all," he said, studying the picture.

"That's a relief," Soapy said thankfully. "Man, I was worried."

Chip laughed. "*You* were worried! How about me?"

"Hey, how about all of us?" Morris demanded.

There was a deep silence until Terring turned away from the picture. "I can't see any sort of a break or chip," he said. "Of course, there's a lot of swelling. I'll give you a prescription to reduce the swelling, and then we'll take another X-ray. You'll be sitting out of practice for a couple of days, and then we'll reevaluate that elbow."

Rockwell arrived just in time to hear Terring's diagnosis. "Good," he said. Then he turned to Chip. "How is it, Chipper?"

"Not bad."

Terring nodded. "It looks OK, Hank. Lucky!"

Dr. Terring's assistant, Sondra Ruiz, fastened the sling in position. "You wear this until tomorrow afternoon, young man. Now get out of here. All of you!"

Rockwell and Terring were good friends and true sportsmen. Each appreciated the responsibilities of the other, and they often shared their problems.

"Now what?" Terring demanded.

Rockwell sighed wearily. "Same old thing. Two leaders! Two factions!"

"Too many good ballplayers, maybe," Terring suggested.

"Could be!"

"What happened?"

"Well, it was partly my fault. You know what I've been trying to do with Byrnes. Today, I made him pitch to the batters, and he couldn't take it. For some reason he's feuding with Chip."

"Jealousy!" Terring said tersely.

"Anyway, he was sulking, and when I told him to put something on the ball, he lost his head and began throwing wild and hit Chip. I don't think Byrnes is malicious, but it looked as though he didn't care whether he hit Chip or not."

"And?"

"Well, I didn't do anything until after practice. Then I asked him to stop in the office before he showered, and I tried to find out what was going on."

"Any success?"

"Not a bit. He clammed up and wouldn't talk. I got nowhere and had to let him go. Then, when I started over here, I saw something that really worries me. Most of the kids were in here, as you know. But Nickels, Gillen, Burke, and Emery were waiting for Byrnes. I don't like it."

"It doesn't look good," Terring admitted.

While Rockwell and Terring were discussing the problem, Byrnes and his friends were talking about what had happened in Rockwell's office.

"Was he mad?" Emery asked.

Byrnes shrugged. "How do I know? What do I care?"

"He must have been! What did he say?"

"He asked me why I lost my head in the first game and why I was sulking. Lots of nonsense like that."

"What did you tell him?"

"Didn't tell him anything! Why should I? I had nothing to tell! That is, nothing he'd like very much."

Darrin Nickels had been listening to the conversation. He spoke for the first time with just a bit of anxiety in his voice. "Did you really hit him on purpose, Lefty?"

Byrnes grunted. "Well, maybe not on purpose, but—" He hesitated and then continued passionately, "I hate that guy!"

Jim Collins stopped by Grayson's that evening to see Chip and to find out how badly he was hurt. This time, he barged right into the storeroom. Chip was pleased by the visit, and Collins left wearing a big smile. Jim was Chip's number-one fan!

After Collins left, Chip fell deep in thought. He was thinking about Lefty Byrnes, Darrin Nickels, Bob Emery, Ellis Burke, and Murph Gillen. Chip figured it was about time he straightened things out with those five. They had him puzzled. Four were regulars and had no worries about holding their positions. But Lefty Byrnes ranked at the top of the pitching staff. Chip tried to recall any time when he might have offended any of them. He couldn't remember a single incident.

"Byrnes is the leader, all right," he muttered. "No doubt about it. But why is he so bitter?"

Chip was sure of one thing. A pitcher concentrated on the strike zone when he threw a ball; he didn't keep looking at the batter before, during, or after he threw to the plate. He wasn't going to say anything about that to anyone. But he wasn't going to be a fool and get all banged up just because a couple of guys had it in for him. He could play rough, too, if he had to! The first chance he got he was going to have an eye-to-eye showdown with Lefty Byrnes.

Henry Rockwell was doing some thinking too. Rock had exhausted his patience with Lefty Byrnes. He realized he had jeopardized the athletic career of one of the top athletes in the country by trying to rehabilitate a spoiled star.

Rockwell mused, "I knew all along Byrnes was jealous of Chip, and I let things get out of hand. Nickels's return throw might have been deliberate, but I don't think it was malicious. He was probably trying to annoy Chip, not hurt him. But Byrnes's beanball throw had all the signs of an intentional pitch."

In the end, Rockwell made up his mind that he'd almost had enough of Lefty Byrnes. The unruly pitcher was going to get exactly nowhere with those tactics. Byrnes was going to sit for a game or so, and if the temperamental southpaw wanted to do a little growing up while he was sitting, that would be all right too. Maybe he should sit out as long as Chip was out.

Tuesday afternoon, Chip waited impatiently for Dr. Terring. His arm felt much better, and a lot of the swelling had disappeared. When Terring arrived, he brought Chip directly to his private office and carefully examined the elbow. "Coming along nicely, Chip," he said with a pleased smile. "Let's take another picture."

"Doc, the first regular game of the season is scheduled for tomorrow afternoon," Chip hinted.

Terring's face softened. "So I hear. I'm sorry, Chip. You'll have to forget baseball for a while."

"But Doc, my arm feels fine. I—"

Terring stopped him. "Chip, you've got years of baseball ahead of you. I know you don't want to risk permanent injury to your arm just for the sake of a little bit of patience. Right?"

Chip's face expressed his disappointment. "I'd just like to keep in shape, Doc. I'd get flat if I didn't get some work in."

Terring smiled understandingly. "I know, Chip. Don't worry. You'll be back in uniform just as soon as it's practical for you to work out. OK?"

It wasn't OK, but Chip couldn't do anything about it. He headed for Jeff with a heavy heart, hoping to get in a little studying before going to work. But he couldn't keep his thoughts away from baseball and soon headed for Grayson's. Later, when Soapy punched in for work, he told Chip about practice. Nickels had been the only one of Byrnes's friends who had asked how Chip was doing. But it was Cohen who Soapy wanted to talk about.

"Biggie was in rare form today, Chip," Soapy said in admiration. "I never saw him like he was today right after practice. We were all dressing, and it was kinda quiet, and Biggie stood up and rapped on a locker with his spikes and started talking. He said baseball was a great game, but if players couldn't play without pulling mean and dirty tricks, it wasn't worthwhile.

"Everyone was surprised, and there was silence and lots of eyes looking down at their shoes. Then Biggie said that if anyone in the room wanted to do any beanball throwing or dirty sliding or bat throwing or anything, he was ready. Man, you never heard a place so quiet in your life! I think it was the longest speech Biggie's ever made. I never saw him so mad and determined. It even scared *me!*"

Chip sat on the bench for the Southwest State game, but he wasn't in uniform. Rockwell started Flash Sparks on the hill and Soapy behind the plate. Sparks got off to a good start, striking out the first two men he faced and forcing the third to pop a fly to right. Flash was way ahead of the Bisons' hitters and far too fast for them.

In the Fence Busters' half, Crowell walked, Morris sacrificed, and Emery smacked a double to right. Crowell scored. Cohen looked at a curve and then blasted a hopping fastball over the right-field fence. That set the fans to yelling "Fence Busters!" again. Then Burke accentuated the positive by driving the first pitch deep into left field for a three-bagger. The Bisons called time and sent in another hurler. It didn't help. Durley singled, and Murph Gillen punched a double into right-center and went on to third when the throw to the plate got away from the Southwest receiver.

That was the way it went the whole game. It wasn't much of a ball game, but it was action. The fans liked it, and the freshman players gleefully fattened up their batting averages. By mutual consent before the game, Rockwell and the Bison coach had agreed to call the game at the end of the seventh if either team was ahead by twelve runs. The Fence Busters were on their way, winning their first regular game of the season 28-4, and they sent the fans home talking.

Rockwell had used Sparks for four innings and called on Silent Joe Maxim for the last three. Soapy had caught the entire seven innings. Lefty Byrnes and Darrin Nickels watched the entire game from the bullpen.

Chip had arrived at the game with a sling holding his arm; he left with it stuffed in the pocket of his State jacket. Chip figured it might help if his arm got a little exercise. Dr. Terring took another X-ray on Thursday, and his face was one big smile when he finished reading the negative. He turned to meet Chip's hopeful eyes. "Nothing to worry about now, Chipper. Just a matter of time."

Chip breathed a deep sigh of relief. "Then my arm is all right?"

"Well, I wouldn't say that. But you might be able to start working out in about seven to ten days."

"Ten days!"

"That's right. And—"

"But I *can't* wait that long, Doc. There's a game Saturday."

"I know. And there will be another game the following Saturday and the next and the next. Probably a game this time next year too! There'll be lots of games and lots of Saturdays. Now you listen to me."

Chip listened. And he sat it out. He sat in the dugout and suffered as only a baseball player can suffer when he can't play the game he loves.

Rockwell let Byrnes sit too. He gave him the silent treatment and completely ignored the southpaw. Byrnes wasn't worried when he was overlooked the first game, but when the second passed and then the third and he wasn't used, he began to get restless and nervous. Rock would have found Byrnes's efforts to get attention amusing if he hadn't been so worried about the boy. Byrnes reported early to practice, hustled, talked it up, and nearly tore the glove off of Nickels's hand when he warmed up.

Byrnes got his chance in the Baxter College game, and the southpaw worked beautifully, getting nine strikeouts and giving up only six scattered hits. The Fence Busters won easily, 18-1.

Dr. Terring gave Chip the green light on Monday, April 7, and then he broke the bad news. "No throwing with your right arm for four weeks. And no pitching for another two weeks after that."

Chip was demoralized and speechless. "Oh, *no!*" he breathed. "Not for the season?"

CHAPTER 11

One Bad Apple

STATE'S TEAM physician had more than a professional interest in the university's teams and athletes. He liked sports for sports' sake, and he liked college students. Terring, D. H. "Dad" Young, director of athletics, and Hank Rockwell were close friends. Young had known Rockwell for years, and he had been instrumental in bringing the veteran coach to the university. So it wasn't strange that these three men, so much alike in their approach to sports, should be friends.

Terring was worried about Chip Hilton, not because of the injured elbow, but because of the hurt in his eyes. It was on his mind so much that he shared his concern with his wife, Ginny.

"Real tough," Terring said abruptly. "A real tough break."

"What's that, Mike? Another broken leg?"

"No, but I just about broke someone's heart."

"Now, Mike—"

"No, seriously. A baseball player, Chip Hilton. I had to cut off his arm, so to speak. I virtually cut out his baseball for a while."

"You mean the young pitcher who did so well against the varsity?"

"That's the one. Hank's going to be sick when he hears about it. I think I'll call him. I'll call Dad too."

"But your dinner, Mike?"

"Can't eat right now. Sorry. You mind?"

"Of course not."

Henry Rockwell had missed Chip at practice, and he had missed Terring on the way home. But he suspected the worst and was just about to call Terring when the phone rang. It was Mike, and he and Dad Young were coming over. Nothing to worry about, he explained. They just wanted to talk to him.

"Chip?"

"In part," Terring said gently. "Now don't worry. It's nothing serious."

Dad Young had been at State a long time; he had survived several administrative and athletic changes, and the students, faculty, and alumni all loved him. Young stood by his coaches, realizing that a coach was only as good as his players. He had watched the varsity and freshmen in the campus series and had been disgusted with Byrnes's behavior. The information Mike Terring had given him had added to his dislike for the temperamental pitcher.

Rockwell greeted his two friends anxiously. "Chip's arm?" he queried.

"The arm is coming along fine, Hank," Terring assured him. "We just wanted to talk to you about Chip's attitude and how he's dealing with the arm."

"And about a couple of your other players," Young added.

"But what about Chip?"

"He shouldn't do any throwing at all for about four weeks, Hank, and no pitching for a couple more. It'll be about six weeks, I'd say, before he'll be able to pitch a game." He made a hopeless gesture. "I'm sorry. But that's only part of it. What I really wanted to talk about was the kid's heart. What I had to tell him today— well, it hurt him a lot. He tried not to show it other than giving the usual protests you'd expect from an athlete who loves baseball, but he was way down when he left my office."

"Mike and I were wondering if the kid couldn't work out," Young interjected. "Run, chase down flies, maybe do a little hitting and running. He's a great kid, Hank. Quite a contrast to many of the *star* athletes we see in colleges and universities these days. Most of them have been over-publicized and pampered and spoiled until they think the world owes them everything served on a platter.

"Chip's never asked the Athletic Department for a single thing, and I'm certain he could qualify for financial assistance or a general scholarship. And next year we'll offer him a varsity athletic scholarship, but I think I know the answer he'll give us. No, he's an independent kid and works and pays his own way. He's the real thing."

Rockwell smiled. "You're telling me," he said softly.

"Mike and I have been talking about Byrnes and the player split that has developed," Young went on. "You know, Hank, maybe some projects just aren't worth salvaging. I watched Byrnes in that first game, and if I had been in your shoes, I'd have dropped him on the spot. He's a bad apple."

"He must have *some* good qualities, Dad. He works nights delivering pizzas. A kid can't be really bad who works when he really doesn't have to—"

Young stopped him. "Now, just a minute, Hank. Let me get this off my chest. Byrnes has certain qualities that endow him with a type of leadership that unthinking followers sometimes confuse with the real thing.

"If you want to drop him or suspend him, I'll support it. He's trouble! Remember, this pilot program is supposed to make a difference, but I don't expect miracles from all my coaches every day. Now I've had my say, and the rest is up to you."

"But Byrnes has changed," Rockwell insisted. "I think he actually felt bad about Chip. He's hustled and acted like a different person ever since."

Mike Terring had kept quiet. Now he spoke. "Let me ask you a couple of simple questions, Hank. First, has Byrnes ever said one thing to Chip? Has he ever expressed any regret to the kid he knocked out of baseball?"

Rockwell shook his head, "Why, I don't—"

"Well, I do!" Terring interrupted. "Now let me answer my own questions. Neither Byrnes nor any of the other four in his group has said a single word to Chip. And, according to all the information I can get, none of the five has ever expressed a bit of regret that the kid can't play. Now you mark my words. As soon as Chip comes back out for that team—as soon as he's able to pitch and starts to pitch the way he can—you'll have trouble with Byrnes again."

"I agree with Mike," Young said firmly. "Byrnes has to be the whole show and the only show, or he'll break up the act."

The three friends talked for another hour, and after Young and Terring departed, Rockwell took off for Grayson's. He found Chip in the storeroom, his nose buried in a history book. Rock was there only fifteen minutes, but when he left, Chip's eyes were bright again, and he could hardly wait for the next day and practice.

Gee-Gee Gray broke the Hilton story that evening during his seven o'clock sportscast. Among the interested listeners was Lefty Byrnes.

"Yes, Chip Hilton was expected back in action this week, but Dr. Terring put a damper on that and placed the brilliant pitcher on the shelf for six weeks.

"Hilton will be missed not only for his pitching, but also for his prowess at the plate. But his loss—aside from the brilliance of his play—doesn't have to be a serious blow. Few, if any, college teams can boast hitters like this freshman fence-busting team. The pitching will be weakened, of course, but their schedule is well spaced, and Rockwell has four capable hurlers in Byrnes, Sparks, Dean, and Maxim."

"Six weeks!" Byrnes exulted. "Now I can make them forget there ever was a Chip Hilton!"

Jim Collins heard the broadcast and drove to University to see Chip. He knew how a player felt when he got a six-week setback in baseball. He looked at the gnarled fingers of his throwing hand several times on the way. A broken thumb, a forefinger that was still crooked, and enlarged knuckles on all of his fingers attested to the hazards of playing behind the bat.

A lot of Chip's other friends felt the same way, but they didn't know how to express their thoughts and feelings.

"It isn't so bad," Chip told them cheerfully. "Dr. Terring said I could work out. I'm just thankful not to have a break or chip."

Byrnes and his crowd were shocked when Chip showed up in the locker room Tuesday afternoon and suited up for practice.

FENCE BUSTERS

"I thought he was out for six weeks," Burke said incredulously.

"Probably gonna coach the pitchers," Nickels said mischievously, eyeing Byrnes.

"That's not even funny," Byrnes growled.

Chip acted as if nothing was different during practice except that he threw and lobbed the ball around with his left hand. He ran the bases and chased flies and even took a turn sliding—practicing the hook on his left side, hooking with his right foot, and keeping his right arm out of trouble.

The fans were surprised to see Chip in uniform when they turned out for the Crampton Community College game. The Tigers had a veteran lineup and had won the junior college championship the preceding season. If rural boys are natural ballplayers, then Crampton, located in the heart of the farming belt, was going to have success for many seasons to come.

Rockwell started Silent Joe Maxim, and the Fence Busters found out in the top of the very first frame that they weren't going to push these Crampton players around. The Tigers' batters teed off on Joe and drove in four runs before the State freshmen could get them out. But four runs meant nothing to the Fence Busters, and they came hustling in, anxious to get hold of their favorite bats and punish the ball.

The Crampton pitcher was a big freshman who simply reared back and gave every pitch everything he had, then he forgot what happened next. He was fast and wild. The Fence Busters liked to dig in, plant themselves solidly in the batter's box, and get set to bust the fences. They didn't dig in on this Tiger. Maybe the first time and for the first pitch, but after that, they stepped up cautiously and were always prepared to duck or get out of the way.

ONE BAD APPLE

Crowell walked after ducking, twisting, and dodging four weird throws. Ozzie had no chance to do anything but walk. Speed Morris was a natural choice for the second spot in the batting order as he was an excellent push-along hitter. But a push-along hitter has to have a chance to get wood or metal on the ball or a chance to bunt. Or at least try! Speed didn't have the chance. The hurler was evidently trying to keep his pitches high or inside or both, or maybe he was just inaccurate. At any rate, Speed walked too.

Bob Emery was a left-handed hitter. He stood in the rear of the box and blasted away. He was anxious to maintain his .500 average and swung from the heels at the wild pitches. And the Tiger struck him out.

Biggie Cohen liked to hit fastballs, and that was all the Tigers hurler was throwing. But he was throwing all over the place. Biggie ducked and dodged four wild throws and landed on first, filling the bases. That brought up Belter Burke. He tried to live up to his nickname and went for the wild pitches. They were all bad, but Belter managed to connect with one he had to hit or get hit by and drove a screamer skipping along the ground to the right of the shortstop.

The Tigers infielder made a spectacular stop, smothered the ball, dropped it, picked it up, and fired it to second in time to nip Cohen. The throw to first caught Burke for the double play to retire the side. So the Fence Busters took the field without any runs and with just a little bit of apprehension filtering through their cockiness.

The Tigers started right in again and scored two runs before they were retired to lead 6-0. And when the Fence Busters came in to hit in the bottom of the second, the fans were yelling for some runs.

FENCE BUSTERS

Andre Durley liked to crowd the plate. The big, wild pitcher fixed that, and quick! He unleashed a fastball that Andre couldn't dodge, and the ball plunked into Durley's broad back between his shoulder blades. Rockwell called time.

After making sure that Durley was all right, Rockwell complained bitterly to the umpire about the dangerous pitching. He had a lot of support from the fans. The coach always has the hometown fans behind him in an argument with the visitors.

The aggressive Crampton coach stalked out on the field and wanted to know what was wrong with the "great hitters" he had heard so much about. "Want us to throw underhand or give your guys a tee?" he taunted.

"We don't want to get killed up there," Rockwell retorted.

"Play ball," the umpire ruled. "I don't know whether he knows where the plate is, but I do know he couldn't hit anyone if he tried. Play ball!"

Murph Gillen hit from the first-base side of the plate, but the right fielder didn't come close to hitting the Tigers pitcher. The first pitch sent him sprawling in the dust, and he never recovered. He struck out on three bad ones and stomped his way back to the dugout after slinging his bat angrily in that direction.

Darrin Nickels, a right-handed hitter, always settled his 230 pounds comfortably in the box and waved a massive bat menacingly at the hurler. He waved it this time too. Once! That was his last chance. The ball came whistling in, and Darrin sat down. Fast! After that, the big bruiser of a batter was wary. He thought more about ducking than hitting. But he swung mightily at one of the mad throws, and the result was a high fly that the Tigers second baseman gathered in behind the keystone bag.

ONE BAD APPLE

Joe Maxim had a lot of courage. The big freshman played tackle in football, and moving him was like trying to budge the Rock of Gibraltar. If Silent Joe had been a little faster on his feet, he would have made a fine first baseman or outfielder. But Rockwell was using Rico Williams as the designated hitter.

Rico threw and batted right-handed, and he was determined to hit the ball. He was also worried about those six runs and couldn't wait to catch up. Rico managed to get a piece of a bad ball, popping it up to the first baseman for the easy third out. And so the Fence Busters had been blanked two innings in a row for the first time in the young season.

By all rights, the big visiting pitcher should have tired as the game wore on. He should have tired or started throwing the ball away, or gotten flustered with the men on the bases. Or something! But he didn't!

Sparks came in for Maxim in the fourth, but it didn't seem to make much difference to the Crampton Tigers. And the longer the game went, the more the big, awkward pitcher seemed to like it. He kept smiling and heaving the ball, and the Fence Busters gritted their teeth and tried harder but got nowhere fast.

The frustrated State freshmen did manage to blast in two runs in the fifth and three more in the seventh, but the Tigers kept adding to their total, and the tempo of the game remained unchanged. When the visitors took the field for the top of the ninth, they were leading 12-5.

The fans were making all the noise they could when the Fence Busters came in for their last at-bat. They were cajoling, pleading, and demanding some runs. Jim Collins was nearly beside himself and had yelled until he was hoarse: first at the big visiting pitcher and then by trying to cheer in some Fence Busters runs.

FENCE BUSTERS

Morris led off in the bottom of the ninth after flashing a worried look at the scoreboard. Speed had walked twice, and the Tigers walked him again. Emery swung at the first pitch, a ball that came in above his head. Somehow he hit it, driving the ball into the outfield gap between the right fielder and the foul line, where it rolled to the fence. Speed scored, and Bob pulled up at third.

Then Biggie electrified the crowd by powdering the first pitch, sending it high over the right-field fence. That made it 12-8 and gave the Fence Busters new life.

The blow brought life to the Fence Busters' fans too. This game wasn't over! The big pitcher was finally tiring! The Fence Busters had just been fooling around with the Tigers! Belter, Andre, and Murph would park the ball over the fence now! The old bats were ringing again! But Burke struck out. Then Durley hit a screamer! There was a crack, a flash of streaking light toward left field, and a long, low moan from the fans. The Tigers shortstop had leaped high in the air, and the ball had stuck, much to the dismay of the State fans. That was two away!

Gillen hadn't touched the ball all day. Now the fans yelled for a pinch hitter and called on Rockwell to do something. Frantically, they pleaded, demanded, and begged him to help the Fence Busters out of this impossible situation.

"Put in Hilton!" a fan behind the dugout yelled in a shrill voice. "He can hit better than that guy with one hand!"

"Hilton," the crowd echoed. "We want Hilton!"

CHAPTER 12

De"fence"less Busters

ROCKWELL ALWAYS hears the crowd. He can't avoid hearing the grandstand advisers barking and bellowing commands for the moves and calling the shots so confidently. But Rockwell didn't intend to put Chip in the game. Byrnes and his sorry followers weren't going to use Chip or anyone else for any kind of an alibi today. That was all over! The Fence Busters had no one but themselves to blame for this debacle, and he didn't intend to let Chip share any part of it. No, Gillen could do his own hitting. Or missing!

Rockwell had no other recourse. He couldn't have used Chip in that game under any circumstances. Not until he had given Chip a chance to work out a few more days and had proved conclusively to himself that the star player could hit a ball without fear of further injury to his arm.

Murph Gillen heard the fans and cast a questioning look in the direction of third base, but Rockwell turned his back and looked out toward left field. It was too late to do anything now but hit away. Gillen was on his own. Murph tried hard, but he struck out on three straight fireballs. The Fence Busters had lost their first game of the season!

The players didn't waste much time vacating the Alumni Field dugout. They left silently and morosely. And there wasn't much talking in the locker room after the game. Each player seemed in a hurry to take a shower, dress, and get away from the scene.

The fans, however, reacted differently. They couldn't seem to realize that the game was over and that the Fence Busters had lost. They moved slowly toward the exits, rehashing the plays and the game.

"That big guy didn't have a thing!" someone said angrily.

"He had a lot of speed," another observed.

"I thought the kids liked fastball pitching," a hurt voice complained.

"Hitting wasn't so bad," a deep voice contended. "It was the errors in the field that whipped them."

A loud-voiced fan summarized the game best of all. "Look! They've been trying to bust the fences every time they go to bat. That's their trouble! They believe everything they read in the papers. They think they can knock every pitch over the fence. And as far as fielding is concerned, they've *never* played good defensive ball. Now it looks like they'll have to learn to play the game the right way."

Bill Bell must have been listening to the last speaker. The sports editor's Thursday morning *Herald* story put it straight.

DE"FENCE"LESS BUSTERS

DE"FENCE"LESS BUSTERS LOSE FIRST
OF SEASON
Freshmen Lose to Crampton 12-8

The de"fence"less Fence Busters lost their first game of the season yesterday afternoon at Alumni Field when Elmo "Rocket" Schlundt, Crampton's elongated pitcher, wrapped and tied up the bats of the locals and stilled the fence-busting ideas of State's heavy-hitting squad to lead the Tigers to a 12-8 upset victory.

If wild swinging and efforts to kill the ball are criteria of fence-busting, then State's first-year wonders lead the field. Reference to *field* does not imply that Rockwell's freshman phenoms know what the term means on a baseball field.

Defense? They have none. Pitchers? They have one. But only when the injured Hilton is on the hill. Power hitting? They have some when opposing pitchers let them dig in and tee off.

Some pitchers don't let hitters have all the privileges. The Tiger "Rocket" Schlundt belongs in that category. If Henry Rockwell's De"fence"less Busters expect to win the Little Four championship they've been driving for, they had better forget the fences and start trying to meet the ball.

Wesleyan brings both its teams here Saturday. Game time for the freshman game is ten o'clock. The varsity game is at 2:30.

Chip was raring to go when he reported to practice on Thursday. So was Jim Collins. He was taking the responsibility of hitting to the outfielders seriously and had brought his own bat. The eager fan was the first

FENCE BUSTERS

person on the field. Chip joined in shagging Collins's long flies. But this time there was a difference. Chip was concentrating hard on his left-handed throws back to the fan. He was pegging them in just the way he would in a game—low and fast and hard and on the first bounce.

The infielders had the first practice hits, and when the outfielders came in for their turn, Rockwell called Chip.

"Arm strong enough for a little hitting, Chip?"

"Feels fine, Coach."

"All right, take a turn."

It was all right. Chip took his turn and met the ball with solid, ringing blows. Rockwell watched the hitting until he was satisfied that Chip could hit the ball without flinching. Diz Dean was serving up the practice throws, and he laid them in perfectly for batting practice.

Chip was driving the ball hard and straight. The ball took off on a straight line, kicking up the dust between the infield and the outfield, skipping hard, clear to the fence. Chip could hit to all parts of the field and switched from the left to the right side of the plate on each of his hitting turns.

The pitchers had been chasing the hits, and when Rockwell sent the outfielders out to chase, he called for the pitchers to come in and hit. Byrnes waited in the line of Chip's path at second base, fumbling with his shoelace until Chip passed by.

"Faker," Byrnes gritted, keeping his voice low. "Who do *you* think you're fooling with that injured elbow act?"

Chip turned and came back. "I'm not trying to fool anyone about my arm, Byrnes," he said coolly. "I hope you don't think you fooled me when you threw that beanball."

"Thought you got hit in the arm, faker."

DE"FENCE"LESS BUSTERS

"I did," Chip said evenly. "But you aimed at my head, didn't you?" He looked the ill-natured pitcher directly in the eyes. "That's dirty baseball, Byrnes. And *you* know it!"

Byrnes shifted his eyes and turned away. But he couldn't resist one last barb. "Rockwell's grandstander who likes to fake," he hissed. "Hard to be a star with a bum arm, isn't it, grandstander?"

Chip was tempted to follow Byrnes. But he didn't want to attract the attention of his teammates and start a fight on the diamond, so he continued on to the outfield. He tried to figure it out for the thousandth time. What was it all about? This feud had gone far enough! He'd have a face-to-face talk with Lefty Byrnes the first chance he got! The sooner the better. He'd show Byrnes the "bum arm" too.

Chip really leveled off on Friday. He was feeling right and got a bit further under the ball, sending it far and high, often over the fence. Right then he opened his teammates' eyes with his power hitting.

Except for Rockwell and his high school buddies, his teammates hadn't seen Chip really put the metal to the ball. Chip had decided to go all out. He had held back as long as he could. Hurt and puzzled by the injustice of the whole thing, Chip was now fully determined and committed to being the best ballplayer on the field. He laced the ball with all the smoothness, timing, and power at his command.

Biggie Cohen and Darrin Nickels had more weight, but they lacked the smoothness and wrist snap that enabled Chip to flash his bat through at the last instant to give the barrel the all-important last-second impetus, which increases the speed of the bat to and through the ball.

FENCE BUSTERS

The Wesleyan freshmen arrived in town Friday night, and some of the players drifted into Grayson's after they had settled into their hotel. One of the players recognized Chip and spoke to him.

"Playing baseball, Hilton?"

"Trying to, but college ball is tough. Glad to see you guys are here. We've heard you have a good ball club."

"I heard the same about you," one of the boys retorted. "Been hearing a lot about the Fence Busters!"

"The last time we saw you was in a basketball uniform," the other boy smiled. "The night you knocked us out of the tournament."

Chip nodded. "We had a good team. Don't forget you gave us the same treatment here."

"Yeah, but you didn't play here, and you got twenty-eight points on our floor."

"Anyone can get the points when he gets all the shots," Chip remonstrated.

"Yeah, right!" the taller of the two boys said with a grin. "You playing tomorrow?"

Chip shook his head. "Nope. Wish I were."

The visitors grinned. "Good!" the smaller player said. "Maybe we'll win one!"

It was good kidding, and Chip liked it. He remembered the basketball trip very well. Wesleyan had been the first of three road games right at the end of the basketball season. All had been must games. Losing any one of the three would have eliminated State from the tournament. But the freshmen won them all and came back to win the tournament.

Chip hadn't forgotten the collegiate athletic hospitality and the friendly spirit of the Wesleyan players and students. The game had been bitterly fought, but when it was over, after the outcome had eliminated Wesleyan and kept State in the running, no one would ever have known Wesleyan had been a contender. No griping, no alibis, no hard feelings. Nothing but praise and good wishes for the winner! That was what sportsmanship was all about.

Jim Collins had been aware of Byrnes's animosity toward Chip for a long time. He had watched the two on the field on Thursday and had decided to try to do something about their differences when he noticed their confrontation at second base. He didn't have a chance until Friday evening when he surprised Lefty Byrnes at Peppi's Pizza Parlor.

"Hi, Lefty. How's business?"

"Good, Mr. Collins," Byrnes said cheerfully.

"You pitching tomorrow?" Collins asked.

"It's either me or Dean," Byrnes said shortly. "Or at least it should be. Maxim and Dean worked Wednesday."

Collins saw the opening and cleverly took advantage of the opportunity. "Too bad Hilton can't help you guys out," he said sympathetically. "You need a couple more pitchers. There's too many games this early in the season."

Byrnes laughed scornfully. "Hilton? That grandstander?"

"Grandstander!" Collins echoed. "I never figured Hilton was a grandstander." He studied Byrnes a moment and then said, "Say, what's going on with you and Hilton?"

"I'm particular about the kind of people I choose for my friends," Byrnes said shortly. "I can't stand the guy."

Collins tried unsuccessfully to get to the root of Byrnes's dislike for Chip. But Lefty just wasn't talking about that, and he evaded every leading question. Before Collins said good night, though, he made sure he left the touchy hurler in a good humor by assuring him that the real fans were pulling for him to come through. The last statement wasn't completely genuine, but Collins felt he ought to say something to calm the ruffled freshman. "Hope the team gives you better support than they gave the guys Wednesday," he said kindly. "I'll be pulling for you tomorrow, Lefty!"

Byrnes couldn't get Chip Hilton out of his mind that evening. "I don't get it," he kept saying to himself. "Why does everyone rave about Chip Hilton?"

Byrnes was trying to justify his jealousy of Chip Hilton. He kept telling himself he had to stand up for his rights even if he had to take on the coach and the whole team. Byrnes had to admit that Chip could hit a baseball, and he guessed Rockwell's "pet" had something on the ball as a pitcher, but why all the praise? Byrnes figured it might be left over from the football and basketball seasons. He'd never been much of a football or a basketball player himself, and maybe that had been a mistake.

Lefty just couldn't understand baseball fans. "Hilton comes in and gets some breaks and then meets a ball just right and happens to win a single game, and they think he's the greatest since Roger Clemens," he complained.

A little later Byrnes spotted Nickels and Gillen and took them for a ride on his next delivery. He told them about Collins's visit and about Chip Hilton. "He said we ought to be friends," Byrnes said, laughing loudly. "Can you get that? Get real!"

"Mr. Collins is an OK guy," Nickels said thoughtfully. "He's been nice to us. I like him."

Gillen nodded. "He's cool. He likes us and baseball."

Rockwell and Terring spent the evening at Dad Young's house. Rockwell was full of good news about

DE"FENCE"LESS BUSTERS

Chip's arm. Only a very few of Rockwell's close friends knew the deep respect and love he held for Chip Hilton and the Hilton family.

It was never apparent in their relationship on the ballfield. But Rock couldn't fool his two friends. They understood the bond between the two and appreciated the veteran mentor's interest in the young athlete.

"He's really banging the ball in batting practice," Rockwell said excitedly. "I've always thought Chip would be more valuable to a team as an outfielder than as a pitcher. In fact, he played first base for me one season and worked behind the plate the next. Powdered the ball both years."

"He's some pinch hitter," Terring added. "He always finds a way to get the job done!"

Rockwell started out for Alumni Field the next morning fully determined to use Chip if the opportunity presented itself. Before the game he thought it might be wise to prepare the Fence Busters for the worst, and he held a short pregame clubhouse session. He immediately laid the cards on the table for everyone.

"I thought our lineup was pretty well set," Rockwell began, looking from player to player. He hesitated long enough for that to sink in and then continued. "But we've lost sight of a lot of the things we worked on before the season started. We've been reading all the newspaper ink about being sluggers and, worse, believing it! Time and again I've stressed the importance of stroking the ball, meeting the pitch with a smooth swing, and letting the distance take care of itself. But the second you guys throw away the doughnut and reach the plate, you begin aiming for the fences and wind up in the dugout without ever touching first base.

"I want you to go out there this morning and prove you are thinking in terms of the team and not personal batting averages and home runs. If you don't—" There was a long, tense pause before Rockwell continued. "If you don't, I'll have to make some changes. That's all. Byrnes will pitch, and Nickels will catch. Let's go get the job done!"

The Fence Busters tried hard to play team baseball that afternoon. They used all the inside baseball they had been taught: the advance plays, the bunt, the steal and the squeeze. And they tried to forget the fences. But ballplayers don't cure bad habits as easily as that. No, they have to use the signs and use inside baseball in the games until they become a part of their regular play. The Fence Busters hadn't tried to do anything in the games so far except knock down the fences and each other. So they messed everything up.

Byrnes worked hard, but his support was bad, and Wesleyan got the lead and held it. As the innings rolled on and the visitors stayed out in front, Lefty grew bitter and vented. His teammates didn't give him the support his pitching deserved, and they didn't hit. It wasn't until the bottom of the eighth, with two down and Wesleyan leading 8-5, that the Fence Busters got going.

Cohen walked. Belter Burke smashed a hard grass cutter along the third-base line. The Wesleyan hot-corner guardian barely managed to knock it down, and the ball spun away from his glove. Cohen hit the dirt at second and beat the throw. Burke fairly flew down to first, his long legs eating up the ninety feet as if the distance were sixty. Both were safe.

The fans had long since stopped their futile demands for Chip Hilton when Rockwell electrified them by choosing this time to use Chip as a pinch hitter replacing Murph Gillen. They greeted the decision with a tremendous cheer.

DE"FENCE"LESS BUSTERS

The Wesleyan hurler was a right-hander, and Chip stepped into the first-base side of the batter's box. He worked the count to two and two and then met a letter-high curveball right on the nose. Chip pulled the ball just enough to give him lots of power, and the ball took off over the center fielder's head and then over the fence. The fans cheered him every step of the 360 feet around the bases.

That tied up the ball game at 8-8. Darrin Nickels proved there was still a lot of power left in the State bats by driving the first pitch far over the left-field fence. The Fence Busters were ahead for the first time in the game 9-8. Rico Williams, the D.H., struck out, and Rockwell sent Red Schwartz out to right field and started the home-run hitter for the locker room.

Byrnes seemed to take heart once he was out in front and, in the top of the ninth, blazed his throws in, striking out Wesleyan's designated hitter on four pitches. The second batter, the visitors' peppy second baseman and leadoff man, worked the count to three and one and then dropped a surprise bunt in front of the plate that caught Nickels napping. The little batter was well up the base path before Darrin fielded the ball. Nickels threw before he was set, and the ball sailed high over Cohen's head and carried out into the right-field corner.

Red Schwartz had backed up the play and fielded the ball as fast as he could, but the little runner had scurried around second before Red grasped the ball. Schwartz made a fine throw to third, but the runner slid into the bag ten feet ahead of the ball. Byrnes went dead white and glared at Nickels with frustrated fury. For a brief second it appeared that he was on the verge of duplicating his previous display of temper. But he managed to control himself with a tremendous effort and faced the plate.

The next batter promptly laid down a perfect place-ment to the right of the mound. The runner on third was in with the tying run almost before Byrnes touched the ball. Then, to make it worse, Byrnes's throw to first was in the dirt. Biggie Cohen's long stretch was of no use as the expert bunter beat the pickup by half a step. That brought up Wesleyan's long-ball hitters.

The number-three hitter followed the previous bat-ter's example and tapped the one-and-no pitch to the right of the mound. Byrnes fielded it perfectly, but his hurried throw to second was wild, and both runners were safe.

That did it! Blind with fury, Byrnes threw his glove to the ground and jumped on it. Rockwell called time and hurried out to the mound, motioning for Sparks on the way.

"Too bad, Byrnes," Rockwell said shortly. "You worked a good game. Hit the showers."

Byrnes mouthed something and stalked away, too angry to care about the boos from the crowd. But he got a surprise. The fans hesitated a brief moment and then gave him a solid round of applause. That appeased the angry pitcher for a second, but when he reached the third-base bleachers, his head was down, and he was burning with humiliation and rage. He didn't look up until he reached the left-field gate and almost bumped into Chip Hilton.

CHAPTER 13

Two Peas in a Pod

LEFTY BYRNES and Chip Hilton looked like two peas in a pod. Byrnes was slightly taller and five pounds heavier, but his drooping posture evened the height, and the difference between 185 and 190 was hardly noticeable. The two players stood there silently eyeing each other for a long moment—Byrnes because he was caught by surprise, and Chip because he wanted Byrnes to make the first move.

Byrnes was the first to speak. "Get out of my way, grandstander," he snarled. "We had a winning ball club until you sucked your way back into uniform with your sympathy act."

"How many games did *you* win?" Chip asked softly.

Byrnes's face flooded with anger and resentment. Without warning, he started a vicious hook for Chip's jaw. Chip knocked the left-hand lead aside easily and swung in behind the raging southpaw. Then he clamped his left arm around Byrnes's neck and turned his body sharply to the right, tripping the lefty's body with his thigh. Byrnes fell heavily to the ground, but he was up almost as soon as he had landed. He was up and rushing at Chip with angry curses and swinging wildly.

Byrnes was easy pickings for Chip. The southpaw was a clumsy fighter. He knew nothing about boxing, swung with all his strength, and telegraphed every punch. Chip didn't attempt to hit the reckless Byrnes. He simply slapped and tapped his opponent as he rolled with the punches or ducked the wild blows. Breathing heavily, Lefty suddenly realized Chip was toying with him. He stopped short and dropped his hands, frustrated and almost speechless.

"Why don't you stand up to me and fight?" he managed.

Chip smiled and shook his head, "You don't know how to fight, Byrnes. Besides, there's nothing to fight about. I'd hoped we could talk this thing over—whatever is bothering you! I have no clue what I did to get you mad at me, and I'd like to know what it's all about."

For a second, Chip thought Byrnes was going to rush him again. But the angry freshman dropped his eyes and turned away without answering. There was something pitiful about Byrnes's sudden deflation, and Chip felt sorry for him.

"If I've ever hurt you in any way, Byrnes," Chip said softly, "I'm sorry."

Byrnes made no reply and continued toward the locker room, his head bowed and his legs lagging, his whole body expressing defeat. Chip turned back to see what had happened in the game.

Nothing good had happened. Sparks had forced the first batter to pop up an infield fly that made it two down with runners still on first and second. The Wesleyan catcher, hitting fifth in the batting order, had a good eye and had tagged the ball hard in his previous trips to the plate.

Rockwell signaled for the intentional pass. That filled the bases and brought up the visitors' right fielder. He'd already struck out twice and grounded weakly to second base, and it was good baseball to pass the heavy hitter to get at him. But this time he really tagged the ball. Swinging wildly at one of Sparks's fastballs, the hitter blasted the ball over the right-field fence, and Wesleyan was ahead 12-9. Flash got the next batter on a high fly.

With the heavy end of the Fence Busters' batting order up in the bottom of the ninth, the fans took heart. But Crowell was thrown out on a hard grounder to short, Morris lined a long fly to left field for the second out, and Bob Emery went down swinging. The Fence Busters had now lost two in a row!

Byrnes had showered and was dressing when Chip reached the locker room. There was no one else in the room, but neither spoke. The silence was heavy but not filled with antagonism. It was an uneasy, awkward silence, in which speech would have been jarring one way or another. Byrnes didn't look up but kept his head lowered; his whole attitude was one of despair.

Chip cast one hasty glance at the dejected athlete and hurried into the shower, wishing he could do something—anything—to cheer up this disheartened teammate. Chip had been thinking about Byrnes all the way up the hill. All resentment had left him with Byrnes's sudden collapse. In fact, he felt genuinely sorry for Lefty. *There's something behind all this,* Chip reflected. *Something happened a long time ago, and I had nothing to do with it. If it wasn't me, it would be someone else. What's he need to prove? Why?*

FENCE BUSTERS

Moments later, the Fence Busters came clattering in. State's newest sensations were feeling low. Ballplayers always are when victory has been snatched from their grasp.

Rockwell didn't do much talking Monday and Tuesday, but he had everyone hustling. Reserves had the best time of the season. Mike McGuire took turns with Bob Emery in center field, and Red Schwartz alternated with Murph Gillen in right. Eddie Anderson nearly jumped out of his jersey when Rockwell directed him to a long workout at shortstop. Bebop Leopoulos and Junior Roberts were butterfingered and shocked silly when they worked out on the first team.

The regulars started the game at Midland Junior College and lasted until the eighth. Then Rockwell made his wholesale substitutions. Chip had hit for Emery in the top of the seventh and batted in two runs on a triple to deep right-center. But he died on third and was replaced by Leopoulos when State took the field. The Fence Busters finished the game with a lineup the hometown fans would never have recognized and came back to the campus smarting and completely demoralized after three straight defeats.

The benched regulars came out Thursday expecting the worst and got it—straight from the shoulder. Rockwell kept his reserves in the lineup.

Saturday brought a big turnout for the Southeastern game. Most of the faithful fans arrived early, determined to find out what had happened to their Fence Busters. But they didn't have a chance to analyze the regulars. Rockwell started his revamped lineup. The reserves were short on talent, but they hustled! Silent Joe Maxim worked his arm off, bearing down on every pitch.

The Fence Busters got behind in the third with Southeastern taking a 6-3 lead. In the seventh, with no one out, Schwartz beat out a slow roller to short. Durley hit behind Schwartz, and the ball slipped through the hole into right field. Schwartz tore on around to third, and Durley reached second. Then Rockwell sent Chip in to bat for Junior Roberts.

Chip got a big hand from the stands, but the applause had scarcely slackened when he blasted a fastball over the center-field fence. It was a terrific smash, and the homer carried all of Chip's pent-up determination and power. The three-run homer tied up the game, and that was the score when the Fence Busters took the field in the top of the eighth. The fans had cheered Chip's home run, but they went wild when they saw him trotting out to right field.

"Things will be different now," Jim Collins shouted, all smiles for the first time in days.

"How's he going to throw?" a fan demanded. "What's he going to do when runners get on base? Run the ball in to the pitcher?"

"He'll throw it!" Collins barked. "He can throw the ball a mile left-handed."

"Sure, and so can I."

"I've seen him do it. You wait!" Collins retorted.

They didn't have long to wait. Maxim walked the first hitter and hit the next with a wild pitch. Then the Southeastern cleanup batter connected and drove the ball high in the air clear to the right-field fence. Chip scampered back and waited. The runners waited, too—ready to tag up and waiting for the catch. The fans were standing and watching the drama of this tense situation.

The ball seemed to come off the fence, but Chip gathered it in and began his transfer of glove and ball to his right armpit. The base runners had sprinted with the catch, and the third-base coach had waved the first runner on around third and toward home. Then Chip fired the ball!

The fans watched with eager eyes as the ball came in straight and low for the plate. There was no cutoff on the throw. Not on this one! Everyone in the park could see that the ball was coming in to home plate with a perfect bounce and that it had the runner by twenty feet. That is, everyone but the runner himself. He came in sure of the score until Soapy took the low bounce and easily tagged him out.

The fans were still yelling and jumping up and down when Soapy fired the ball down to third base. The second runner tried a hook slide, but Eddie Anderson tagged him out. It was great baseball, and the stands buzzed.

"What a throw! And left-handed!"

"And all the way from the fence on the first bounce! Came in like a shot!"

"I wouldn't have believed it if I hadn't seen it!"

"What an arm! This kid hits from both sides of the plate and throws with either hand!"

"What's that coach thinking about? That kid ought to be some place in their lineup every game."

"Yeah, someplace or anyplace! Doesn't make any difference to him!"

Up in the broadcasting booth, Gee-Gee Gray had been sputtering all over the place. He couldn't find words to explain the throw. He had been talking about Chip and second-guessing Rockwell, doubting the wisdom of putting a player, an injured player who couldn't throw, in the outfield.

"And . . . and straight as you could imagine, right to the plate on the first bounce. Honest! And it had the runner nailed. I've seen everything now! This kid hits the ball out of the park, bats from either side of the plate, throws with either hand, and pitches a no-hitter! Excuse me, fans, I'm out of adjectives."

Chip's throw to the plate and Soapy's blazing peg to third base broke the visitors' backs. The next hitter struck out, and the score held at 6-6 right down to the last hitter of the game: Chip Hilton!

The Southeastern coach didn't give Chip a chance to be the hero this time. He ordered an intentional pass. Rockwell called time and sent Darrin Nickels up to the plate to bat for Soapy Smith.

Chip danced off first base, teasing the pitcher. It looked as if he was faking, but he went right down on the first throw, a pitchout. The catcher had called the pitch, but he didn't really believe Chip would attempt to steal second. Not on the first pitch! The catcher was ready, and his throw was hard and fast and on the first-base side of the bag. But it was high. Chip slid in on the inside with his right toe hooking the bag and his body falling away toward the pitcher, protecting his right elbow. It was fast and beautiful, and he was safe!

Gee-Gee Gray quit on that one. He simply told his listeners that he had given up, and they'd have to read about this game in the papers.

Now it was up to Nickels. Chip had gotten him ahead of the pitcher and was all set to score. Any kind of a hit would bring him in. Chip kept one foot on the bag, breathing heavily, and waited for the hit. The pitcher checked up on him, went into his stretch, lowered his hands, and checked again. Chip didn't move. But the steal had unnerved the Southeastern hurler, and he missed the plate. Before the next pitch, he checked Chip again.

Chip was standing by the bag, seemingly satisfied, seemingly waiting for the hit.

Rockwell gave Nickels the "take" sign, and the pitcher must have guessed it, because he laid a perfect strike right across the middle of the plate. The catcher grinned and tossed the ball back with an encouraging "Atta baby! Fire it one more time!"

Then Chip moved!

To everyone's amazement, Chip bolted for third base, sprinting madly for the bag. The startled pitcher was absorbed in the hitter; he heard the frantic shouts of his teammates too late. But he whirled and threw the ball—a wild, errant throw that nearly got away from the third baseman. Chip was in with a straight slide, and the crowd went wild. When the cheers died down, a lot of second-guessers criticized the play and the freshman player's wisdom.

"It was a bad play!"

"He could've lost the game! Or been hurt again!"

"Isn't any better on third than he was on second!"

"Bet the coach didn't call that play! Not with two down!"

The last two fans were wrong on both counts. Rockwell had called the play, and a runner is always better off on third than on second! Rockwell knew how Chip could run bases, and he took responsibility for the decision.

The pitcher was rattled now. So was the catcher. Chip charged down the baseline with every pitch, threatening the steal. The count went to three and one. Then the hurler gave up and threw an intentional ball, and Nickels trotted down to first. Ozzie Crowell hadn't hit all day, and Rockwell sent Speed Morris up to bat in his place.

The Southeastern manager visited the mound to calm his pitcher, but it didn't help. He kept throwing to third and watching Chip and worrying. On the two-and-one pitch, Chip did it! He broke for home! And he beat the throw!

That was the ball game. The fans came spilling out on the field and surrounded Chip and his happy teammates. Gee-Gee Gray sat silently above it all, his eyes frozen in disbelief on the crowd below the booth.

CHAPTER 14

Rhubarb Climax

BIGGIE COHEN, Red Schwartz, and Speed Morris walked slowly toward Jeff, rehashing the game and talking about Chip's base-running.

"What's with Chip?" Schwartz demanded. "He's playing like a crazy man!"

"Sure is," Speed agreed. "I never saw him like this! Never saw him so determined to play. I wondered how he'd ever elevate his playing level and ability. Has he been doing something we're not?"

Biggie shook his head. "He shouldn't be playing," he said abruptly. "I'm surprised at Rock."

"You know Chip." Speed grinned. "He'd play if he had to crawl, especially since Byrnes and his crowd got smart."

"He gave me a pep talk last night," Schwartz said ruefully. "He told me I ought to be playing regular and that I had to work a little harder in practice."

Chip was thinking about Red Schwartz at that very moment. Anyone not knowing the inner Chip Hilton would have expected him to be reviewing the game and basking in the thrill of being the star in a great victory. But Chip never spent much time looking over his shoulder. Right now, he was planning a surprise for the team troublemakers, and Red Schwartz was an important part of his plans. Chip was determined to show Byrnes and Company that they weren't the only freshman ballplayers on State's campus.

"Red's a good outfielder," Chip murmured, "and he can hit! I'll get with him again tonight!"

Fireball Finley was the first person Chip saw when he arrived at Grayson's, and that gave him another idea. "Fireball," he whispered jubilantly. "Just what we need, another outfielder!"

Then Chip did something he had never done since he first began to work for George Grayson. Without thinking of the consequences, he reacted just as he would have moved to make a play on the diamond; he made a sudden decision. He stopped in front of the cashier's desk and smiled warmly at Mitzi Savrill.

Mitzi was so surprised she almost forgot to turn on the charm. But she quickly recovered. "I heard all about it, Chip. Congratulations. The boss said you were great!"

"I didn't know Mr. Grayson liked baseball."

"Well, he doesn't follow the game except when one of the staff is playing," Mitzi said stiffly.

"Then he ought to see that Fireball comes out for the team."

"Why?"

"Because Fireball was one of the best high school players in the country. And the team's not doing too well. Remember, I'm not the only one who's injured, and a few guys had to drop out because their grades weren't good enough. Besides, he loves the game. We need him."

Mitzi nodded thoughtfully, "Isn't that a gold baseball Cynthia Ann Collins is wearing?"

Chip nodded, "Sure. How did you know she wears a gold baseball?"

"Women dress for women, Chip."

"Not Cindy! She dresses for Fireball. They've got it bad for each other!"

"Don't *most* girls get their boyfriend's trophies? Don't they?"

Chip debated. "Well, I guess so. But I—"

"Never mind, Chip. You know, I was just thinking that if you had a gold baseball like that—I mean one you could spare—why, I think I might be able to do something about Mr. Grayson and Fireball and baseball."

Chip's smile vanished. He might have known, he told himself. He might have known Mitzi would trip him up some way. He had a gold baseball, all right, but he hadn't figured on giving it to Mitzi Savrill . . . or any other girl. Then he thought of Byrnes and Rock and the Little Four championship, and that did it.

"OK," Chip said lamely. "It's a deal."

Mitzi smiled. "That's all right, Chip," she drawled softly. "I never wear sports jewelry. But thanks anyway."

Chip's ears were a bright red when he passed the fountain. He knew he was not even near Mitzi's league. Sports he understood, but Mitzi was an enigma. He didn't dare glance at Fireball, but he heard the little phony cough and the knowing chuckle. He was in for it now.

Mitzi Savrill was deep in thought the next morning when George Grayson walked past the cashier's desk. And for the first time that he could remember, Mitzi's cheery "Good morning, Mr. Grayson" was lost in a far-away look.

Halfway to the office, Grayson's steps slowed, and he

turned back. Mitzi was a most important member of Grayson's, and George Grayson was concerned about anything that bothered her. He stood quietly in front of the counter, studying the girl. Something was wrong. He tapped gently on the counter. "Why the forlorn face?"

Mitzi was startled. Her eyes flashed wide in surprise. "Mr. Grayson, you scared me out of my wits."

"Yes?"

"I mean it!"

"I'm sorry, but why the long face?"

"Frankly, I'm worried about the drop in our counter business."

"I've noticed it, but what can be done about that? It's spring, Mitzi."

"All the more reason to be worried. This should be the biggest time of the year for that part of the business."

"Well, what's the answer?"

"It's simple. Go back to the principle that made that area the campus center in the first place. Go back to star athletes."

Grayson smiled at Mitzi, "I don't think I need that kind of an attraction. There isn't another store in town with a bigger college crowd."

"Why, Mr. Grayson! Now I *am* surprised. I thought you knew that women spend 80 percent of the nation's income."

Grayson grinned wryly. "Ummm . . . so?"

"College women like being sports stars and being around sports stars."

"Looks like we've got a corner on that department with Hilton and Smith."

"But, Mr. Grayson, how about Finley? He was all-state, and the big-league scouts all chased him. Why not have *three* baseball stars on the payroll?"

"What's this supposed to be, the State Athletic Department?"

"No, just the biggest sports center in town. And it ought to be kept that way. John Kim can fill in until the rush hour because there's not enough business to keep both him and Bill Porter busy. It looks bad when we aren't hustling."

Grayson threw up his hands. "Hold everything," he said defensively. "You win! Just what do you want me to do? How soon will I be hiring female athletes to work with Smith, Hilton, and Finley? Mitzi, I may have to open another business so you'll be able to give jobs to people." His voice was harsh and distraught, but he was grinning. He was still grinning when he climbed the steps to his office. "I just better be sure she's always working for me and not the competition," he mused to himself.

Chip usually took it easy on Sundays except for church and his books. But not this Sunday. He sought out his Valley Falls friends and Eddie Anderson, Junior Roberts, and Bebop Leopoulos and charged into all of them about the way they were playing ball.

"No one has a lock on a starting spot," Chip said aggressively. "You know that! Rock will play the best man no matter whether it's the first game or the last. And don't tell me anything about having to be twice as good as the others. I know that as well as you do. Come on! Let's start tomorrow afternoon!"

Soapy summed it up when Chip left for the library. "Seems to me it's pretty important to Chip," he said significantly. "Guess some of the Fence Busters are in for a surprise. Anyway, I know one five-cent guy who's in for some amazement."

Biggie snickered. "A nickel's worth?"

"Yeah, a Darrin Nickels's worth!" Soapy retorted.

Fireball Finley got a surprise Monday morning when he received an urgent call from George Grayson. He got another when Grayson told him he had heard about Fireball's baseball playing, and he'd like it very much if Fireball would report for the team that afternoon—and *make it!*

A lot of people were surprised that afternoon. Fireball surprised Rockwell by reporting and squelching any doubt about his baseball ability by smashing the ball all over the field and even a few over the fences. His timing was off, but his performance was enough to prove he knew what to do with the bat. Now for the ball.

In the outfield, Fireball caught everything Jim Collins hit that came anywhere near him. That nearly floored Collins. He hadn't even known Finley played baseball. That took care of the bat and the ball.

Finley was fast. He had proved that in football. Collins's daughter could have told her dad all about Fireball, but she had wanted him to form his own opinions about her friends—especially this friend.

Anyway, Chip and Rockwell were two of the few who knew that Fireball could run the length of a football field in full uniform in a little over ten seconds.

Inside, Chip was bursting with excitement, but no one would have known it from the expression on his face. He hustled grimly every second, and every time Red Schwartz glanced at his buddy, he got a big scowl. That was enough for Schwartz. He caught fire and surprised Rockwell and everyone else by moving into Belter Burke's left-field position during practice and demonstrating he was a determined candidate for the outfielder's job. Soapy was never better with the stick or behind the plate.

It was a surprising afternoon. Eddie Anderson was outstanding at shortstop, and Speed Morris, who had been at that position since the first day of practice, quickly got serious. Bebop Leopoulos, Fireball Finley, Red Schwartz, Junior Roberts, and Chip played like angels in the outfield.

Belter Burke, Bob Emery, Murph Gillen, and Darrin Nickels all were nursing bad tempers when practice ended. Lefty Byrnes didn't have to lead their usual gripe session, which turned into an afternoon pity party.

"What's going on?" Burke demanded. "What's got into those guys?"

"What do *you* think?" Emery retorted. "Hilton's been working on the coach. Anyone can see that! Finley works at Grayson's, doesn't he?"

"Could be," Burke said thoughtfully. "What do you think, Lefty?"

"I don't know," Byrnes said shortly.

Nickels and Gillen said nothing. Darrin Nickels was beginning to doubt he really was the number-one catcher on the Fence Busters, and Gillen was thinking Chip Hilton was hitting and fielding too well for him to be sure of his right-field job.

Lefty Byrnes was strangely quiet. He was trying to analyze his feelings toward Chip Hilton. Lefty was disturbed by his reaction in the one-sided scuffle following the Southeastern game. He couldn't understand why he had quit. Byrnes was no coward, and his hatred toward Chip Hilton was deep-seated. But the desire to fight Hilton had disintegrated almost as soon as he realized that Chip had no desire to hurt him. It was hard to fight someone who was trying to reason with him—especially when Chip was demonstrating he could whip Lefty with one arm!

Byrnes was thinking about Chip's footwork and his clever boxing. He could feel the flush of embarrassment creeping up the back of his neck and into his face as he thought of his wild blows and clumsy efforts. "He acted almost like he was handling a baby, a big baby," Byrnes muttered.

Nickels looked at him curiously, "What did you say, Lefty?"

Byrnes made no reply. Nickels and the others exchanged puzzled glances. This wasn't the Lefty Byrnes they had grown to know. Other times and days like this, Lefty had lashed out bitterly just at the mention of Chip Hilton's name. Everything seemed out of focus all at once. Each of the boys loved baseball, and each suddenly realized he might have a fight on his hands to stay on the team.

They found out Wednesday afternoon after the short bus ride to York Junior College. Rockwell called out the batting order in the locker room, and they suddenly knew they had a real fight on their hands.

"We'll hit this way," Rockwell said briskly. "Crowell, second base; Anderson, shortstop; Finley, center field; Cohen, first base; Hilton, right field; Durley, third base; Schwartz, left field; Smith, catch; Maxim, pitch. Let's go!"

Rockwell was giving the hustlers a chance, and it paid off. The Fence Busters didn't damage York's outfield fences, but they did play smart baseball and won 9-2. Chip had gone three for four, and Fireball had two for three, one of them a home run in the fourth with Crowell aboard to break the 2-2 tie. Joe Maxim went all the way and looked stronger in the bottom of the ninth than in the first.

FENCE BUSTERS

So the Fence Busters chalked up their second victory in a row without the griping sluggers.

Most of the squad joined in the happy singing and joking on the way home in the bus. But not Byrnes, Nickels, Gillen, Burke, and Emery. They were inwardly boiling with jealousy and futility, and all were bitter in their silence. When they showed up at practice on Thursday, the sloppiness of their play and their "don't-care" attitude was so obvious that the rest of the players could actually feel the tension building. Rockwell sensed the crisis and was ready for the showdown.

Matters came to a head when Rockwell told Byrnes to throw for batting practice.

"You throw to the hitters, Byrnes," he said easily.

"I'm pretty wild, Coach," Byrnes gritted. "I might hit one of the regulars."

"That's right, Byrnes," Rockwell agreed, smiling blandly. "On second thought, you'd better chase a few flies. Do you good to do a little running."

"Sure been sitting enough," Byrnes muttered. "Half the night delivering, most of the day in school, and all this time on the bench."

"A little rest doesn't hurt a hard-working hurler."

"Driving a pizza wagon and going to school and playing baseball aren't easy. And keeping eligible too."

"I realize that, Lefty."

"I thought maybe you felt a guy who's a loner and drives around delivering pizzas didn't rate or wasn't good enough. I thought maybe I ought to turn in my uniform."

There was a heavy silence. It seemed almost as though the other players had overheard the conversation and stopped their chatter to listen. It wasn't true, of course, but the shouts and practice noise did seem to quiet down—undoubtedly, because every player on the field sensed what was taking place.

Rockwell took his time making a reply. He studied the trademark on the ball he was holding and delayed his answer. Finally, he began to talk. "That wasn't fair, Byrnes. I admire anybody who works his way through school. I was speaking only about baseball. You see, Lefty, it was my belief that you loved baseball and came to State with the idea of getting an education and playing ball at the same time. That you were looking ahead to big-league baseball. If your studies are suffering because of the time you devote to baseball, well, you ought to drop out. Education is first."

Rockwell paused. Then, tossing the ball in the air and catching it with the same hand a number of times, he continued. "You know, Byrnes, if every hopeful who tried out for baseball made the team, there wouldn't be much glory in wearing a uniform. Some players have to sit on the bench and hope and work and practice until their opportunity comes. The good players have to sit, too, once in a while. They have to be big enough to realize that the others can be given an opportunity to star."

Rockwell's voice was hard and serious as he continued. "You're a fine pitcher, Byrnes. You've got all the tools of the trade. But you're never going to be a great pitcher, the truly great pitcher you can be, until you develop emotional balance and learn to control your temper. I hope—"

Rockwell didn't have a chance to finish the sentence. At least not in Byrnes's presence. Lefty pivoted quickly without a word and headed for the gate. Over by the plate, Darrin Nickels watched his pal stride away. Then, hesitating momentarily, he laid the catcher's glove on the ground and removed the chest protector and shin guards. Although there was no halt in the practice, there wasn't a player on the field who didn't know that Darrin had handed his equipment to Soapy Smith and followed his friend.

Emery, Gillen, and Burke were chasing flies, but they saw Byrnes and Nickels leave. They didn't say anything and made no move to follow; but if one had made a break, the others would have fallen in line.

Soapy and Diz Dean took over for the hitters, and the workout went on as if nothing had happened. But every player realized the fight, which had been brewing all season, had reached its climax.

CHAPTER 15

Hustle Pays Off

BAD NEWS travels fast, and the practice incident became a choice tidbit of gossip for every fan in town. Jim Collins heard about it shortly after supper and decided he'd do something about it. Collins wanted to have a little talk with Lefty Byrnes. He was in luck. Byrnes appeared with the delivery car loaded down with Nickels, Burke, Gillen, and Emery. Lefty braked to a brisk stop and backed the car into the reserved parking space in front of Peppi's Pizza Parlor. Murph Gillen was talking, and everyone was so intently listening to what he was saying that Collins waited quietly.

"No way," Gillen said stubbornly. "I can't. I can't quit! Not when Hilton's going so good."

"What's that got to do with it?" Burke demanded.

"Plenty! He's playing better baseball than I ever did in my life. If I quit now, everybody in school will say I couldn't take it."

That remark chilled Gillen's four listeners and ended the conversation. After a short silence, Darrin Nickels stirred restlessly and cleared his throat. "You think we're doing the right thing?" he asked, addressing no one directly but glancing at Byrnes out of the corner of his eye.

Lefty Byrnes turned to Darrin. "No one asked you to walk out," he said hotly. "Do what you want!"

Nickels remained quiet, and each former player busied himself with his own thoughts. Collins broke the silence, tapping on the windshield.

"Hi, guys," Collins said pleasantly. "Am I interrupting anything?"

"No, Mr. Collins," Nickels said quickly, relief showing in his face. "No! Wait, we're getting right out."

"Hear there was a little difficulty at practice," Collins said lightly.

Pairs of eyes shifted from one friend to another. Collins continued slowly, "There's lots of talk going around about it, and I thought you might like to know." He wasn't speaking directly to Byrnes, but it was clear to all of them the pitcher was the target. "Most of the ones I heard talking seemed to feel you might be making a mistake."

Collins waited for a reaction, but none came. After a brief pause he continued, speaking in a gentle voice. "When a team's going bad, guys, that's when every player on the squad needs to dig in and find even more within himself."

It seemed Collins was talking to himself. Not a boy moved. Collins went on, "I don't like to ask *anyone* for personal favors, but I'd sure appreciate it a lot if you'd all show up in uniform tomorrow." He cleared his throat and waited expectantly.

Darrin Nickels made the first move. He took a deep breath, and then the words came fast and furious. "I guess you know how we feel about you, Mr. Collins. We'd do anything for you. All of us! So far, Lefty and I are the only ones who turned in our uniforms. Murph, Belter, and Bob aren't in it at all!"

Byrnes swung out of the car and walked around to the sidewalk. "Neither are you," he said sharply. "The whole deal is mine, and I can take care of myself." He turned to Collins. "I feel the same way as Darrin, Mr. Collins, but I can't *beg* to get back on the squad."

"Beg to get back," Collins echoed. "Lefty, Coach Rockwell didn't cut you. You made the decision yourself. You simply walked off the field and out of baseball! Isn't that right?"

Byrnes shook his head indecisively. "Well, maybe. I guess," he hedged.

"Well, then," Collins said brightly, "all you have to do is show up tomorrow. That's all there is to it. Right?"

Byrnes shook his head. "It's not that easy, Mr. Collins."

"Why not? Listen, I've got an idea. Suppose I go see the coach myself. Suppose I tell him you made a mistake and that you'll be out there tomorrow playing your heart out. OK?"

Again, Byrnes shook his head. "No, Mr. Collins, I prefer to work it out myself. Thanks though."

Nickels made the better suggestion, "It's our place to go to the coach, Mr. Collins. I don't know about Lefty, but I think I'll be out there tomorrow."

"Me too!" Gillen added.

"We'll work it out," Nickels said softly. "Thanks a lot for your help. You're . . . well, you're a good listener, and we all appreciate your friendship."

Jim Collins drove out to the farm that night with a light heart. Next to the members of a man's own family, there is nothing quite so wonderful as giving a helping hand to a bewildered young adult. Most kids need someone to lean on when they make their first break away from home, and it is in this vital period of their lives that lifelong impressions are made. Collins was the kind of man who made the right impression, and although he was never to know, he was the direct reason for the decision the five young men made shortly after his departure.

The rift in the ranks of the Fence Busters had been common knowledge to all the fans and the sportswriters too. An interested spectator at that Thursday's practice had been Gil Mack. He had followed the fortunes of the Fence Busters ever since the day he had watched the first practice session and given the team its nickname. And Mack had been greatly disillusioned when his Fence Busters fell off in their hitting and began to lose games.

The sportswriter had been a little disgusted when some of the players began concentrating on the fences and their batting averages instead of team play. Mack was on Rockwell's side all the way. He had appreciated the problem and marveled at the patience of the veteran coach. Trying to help, Gil had previously written several sharp columns about the selfishness of the freshman stars. The scene he had observed on Thursday afternoon gave him another chance to pour it on Byrnes and his companions. Mack really went to town the next morning in the *Statesman*.

FENCE BUSTERS
RIFT COMES TO A SHOWDOWN

Lefty Byrnes and Darrin Nickels
Turn in Their Uniforms
by Gil Mack

Coach Henry Rockwell has coached hundreds of young athletes, male and female, in the thirty-odd years he has been in baseball, and he has undoubtedly met a lot of temperamental ballplayers. However, he must feel the present crop of would-be stars that I erroneously tagged the Fence Busters might top them all. Last evening, following the resignation of two disgruntled players, Coach Rockwell stated there wasn't room on the freshman squad, or any State squad, for any athlete who wouldn't hustle.

He's right! There are at least three more regulars who ought to start hustling. The inadequate performance of several regulars is a clear indication that they not only feel it unnecessary to hustle, but believe they can practice when and how they please. Byrnes and Nickels will be missed, but there are other capable players.

Soapy Smith, for instance, is a first-class receiver. The regulars referred to above are Bob Emery, Murphy Gillen, and Ellis Burke. The outfield trio has been resting on their early-season laurels and should be benched.

Going further, it might be wise to give Speed Morris a jolt. The clever shortstop seems to have lost much of the aggressive play that made him a standout in the preseason drills.

A tip of the baseball cap to Coach Rockwell and his avowed determination to limit freshman uniforms to players who want to play hustling baseball.

The story wasn't as critical as it might have been, but it brought a lot of repercussions. Henry Rockwell didn't like it and called Gil Mack to express his displeasure.

Rock felt that Mack had misinterpreted his statement about hustling. Mack's article had been derogatory to the players, and Rockwell was extremely upset. He wasn't the only one who was upset. Lefty Byrnes, Darrin

Nickels, Bob Emery, Murph Gillen, and Ellis Burke were completely demoralized.

The five friends had sorted out their baseball problem after Jim Collins left the previous evening. They had resolved to see Coach Rockwell and forget the past. Lefty Byrnes had gone along with Nickels and had agreed to see Rockwell and ask for another chance. They met for lunch at their usual eating place, but they weren't in the mood for food. Each had read Gil Mack's story. Byrnes was bitterly sarcastic.

"Ask Rockwell for another chance? No way! Never! I wouldn't ask him for anything! I'm glad now we didn't let Jim Collins talk to Rockwell. We would've been fools! Temperamental! Won't be missed! Hustling baseball!"

"No room," Burke snorted. "Would-be stars!"

Darrin Nickels took a different view. The big catcher felt there was some mistake. "I don't believe the coach said that," he mused. "He's not that kind of man. Mack's clever. He can twist words around so that black spells white."

Bob Emery couldn't see that it mattered. "So what?" he asked.

"So we don't play any more baseball," Burke said shortly.

"I do," Gillen remonstrated. "At least, I go out and try! Any of you guys going with me?"

"Let's think about it," Nickels said slowly. "I think we ought to stick together one way or the other."

"There's only one way for me," Gillen said firmly. "I want to play ball. I'm responsible enough to admit I wasn't hustling and that the coach did the right thing. I'm going back."

Gillen meant what he said. He was the only member of the group at practice that afternoon. Surprisingly,

HUSTLE PAYS OFF

their absences drew little or no comment. Rockwell had expected it would turn out that way, and Red Schwartz, Fireball Finley, Soapy Smith, and other team members were far from displeased. And, just like that, something happened to the morale of the ball club. It was evident in the hustle and in the chatter and in the catcalls and in the good-natured insults that flew from player to player.

The hustle and spirit carried over to Saturday morning and resulted in a smashing 7-1 victory over Calvin-Baines College. Fireball Finley led the assault with the bat, getting three for four and playing brilliantly in the field. Schwartz was one for four, but he covered left field like a blanket. Soapy walked twice, flied out to left, and laced a two-bagger to center in four trips to the plate. Chip played the entire game, getting one for two and walking three times. Henry Rockwell breathed a big sigh of relief and grunted with pleasure when it was over.

This was his kind of ball club. For the Valley Falls contingent, it was quite a day. They finally had something to E-mail home about. The game marked the first time all five members had played in the same game.

Speed Morris? It didn't look as if he was going to make it, but he did. In the bottom of the eighth, Rockwell made it 100 percent representation when he sent Speed in to pinch hit for Eddie Anderson.

That Sunday was a memorable one at the Collins farm. It was Cindy's nineteenth birthday, and Fireball was in charge. He had picked the guests. There were six or eight of them, most of them selected from his Valley Falls friends—Soapy, Biggie Cohen, Speed Morris, Red Schwartz—all of them except Chip Hilton. He had been the first to be invited, but someone had to keep the doors open at Grayson's. Even though the afternoon turned

cold and rainy and business was quiet, Chip persuaded
Soapy and Fireball that he could take care of the counter
for them and, at the same time, catch up on some reading for his Shakespeare course.

Fireball had appealed to Mitzi for help, and she had
offered to get her younger sister to come over and help
Bill Porter behind the counter during the afternoon and
evening. Chip couldn't be persuaded, even by Cindy's
father when he came to pick up the crew. Chip saw them
off with a smile and presents for Cindy from him and
George Grayson. He noticed Eddie Anderson and one or
two other players on the freshman baseball team were
crowded in the Collins car.

Chip really didn't know why he had refused the invi-
tation to attend the party. He really loved farms, especially one like the Collinses' with its big barns, rolling
acres, comfortable farmhouse, and warm hospitality.
Mitzi looked at him thoughtfully when he turned back
into the store after seeing Jim Collins and his friends
drive away.

The entire group of freshmen, led by Soapy, sang on
the way and made up in volume what they lacked in har-
mony. Cindy met them at the doorway that led to the
great room that served as the kitchen and family room.
She was wearing a bright yellow blouse, which added
cheer to the dull, cloudy day. It was the color of spring
daffodils, and her lovely face wore a smile to match it.

Biggie Cohen and one or two others went out to the
barns with Jim Collins to help with the chores while the
rest helped Cindy. And somehow, among the noisy confusion and the horseplay, the table got set. Jim Collins and
his aids came stomping in from the chores, and a few
moments later they were all sitting down to an afternoon
celebration.

HUSTLE PAYS OFF

Soapy stared restlessly at the heaped-up platters while Cindy opened her gifts. At last Jim Collins said a short grace, and then they all fell to work on the delicious food that Cindy and Aunt Mary had prepared. It was a happy day, and the polished oak beams of that great room rang with laughter. They missed Chip Hilton, but his absence could not possibly have dampened that carefree afternoon of fun and celebration.

Then Fireball brought in the cake. It was lit by nineteen candles, and Cindy's sweet face hovered above the soft glow of the candlelight, eager to blow them out. One of the boys ran into the living room and began to pound out Happy Birthday on the piano. Everybody stood up and the off-key notes rang out above Cindy's laughter.

And then it happened! Some thought it was a spark from one of the candles that the girl had blown out. Some blamed the doughnut that had hurtled across the table and struck one of the candles. But in an instant Cindy's beautiful blouse was ablaze. She screamed in fright and anguish. Fireball whipped off his jacket and threw it around her, smothering the flames. Jim Collins almost tipped over the table in his hurry to get to his daughter's side. Waving the guys back, he seized the girl in his arms and rushed into the living room. Everyone seemed paralyzed over the sudden disaster. No one spoke. No one moved. Only Fireball seemed to have his wits about him. He raced to the hallway phone near the door. With one bound he reached it and dialed 9-1-1.

Only when he was assured by the emergency dispatcher that the ambulance was on the way did he turn to face the room. His awed teammates saw he was crying. After what seemed like an eternity, they heard the ambulance siren.

FENCE BUSTERS

It was late when the boys got back to town. Jim Collins and Fireball had accompanied the ambulance to the hospital. The group turned out the lights in the now silent room, which only a short time before had been the scene of so much celebration.

Only a few words were spoken on that dark, rainy night as the members of the baseball team made their way back to town.

"I hope she—"

"Second-degree burns. That's awful!"

"How'll we ever face it if—"

"Let's not tell Chip."

"He's bound to find out."

"I wish I didn't ever have to go back to school."

It was late when Chip locked up Grayson's that Sunday night. He had been expecting Soapy and Fireball to stop in on their way home. When they had not arrived by eleven, he turned out the lights and locked up the empty store. He was even more astonished to not find Soapy in their room when he reached the dorm.

When Chip woke up on Monday morning, he found his usually irrepressible roommate strangely subdued. It might have been better if Soapy had confided in Chip what was on his mind that blue Monday morning. The double disaster that hung over the Collins home had left the redhead sick at heart, and he did not want Chip to share in his misery.

While the old fight and hustle was still there when the team took the field against Ramsey College that afternoon, nothing seemed to happen. Finley couldn't hit, and Soapy was worse. Morris and Schwartz tried too hard, and the ever-dependable Biggie could do nothing right.

Chip was murderous with the bat and faultless in the field, but his performance wasn't enough, and the Fence Busters dropped the game by a 6-5 score and hit the bottom of the well in spirits. The Ramsey pitcher didn't have a thing, and Chip couldn't figure it out. Rockwell added to the confusion by sending Murph Gillen up to hit for Cohen in the ninth. It was the first time in Chip's memory that Rockwell had used a pinch hitter for the hard-hitting first baseman. But Gillen's result was the game-ender. He hit the two-and-one pitch right back to the mound for the third out.

Low in spirits and baffled by the sudden collapse of his teammates, Chip couldn't figure it out. What had happened?

Soapy knew the answer. The redhead found it difficult to keep a secret at anytime, but it was almost impossible for him to refrain from telling Chip. Talking to a morose Fireball that evening at work, Soapy broached the thought.

"I oughta tell Chip, Fireball."

"Nothing doing!"

"But why? Speed and Biggie and Red know about it. Why not Chip?"

But Finley was adamant. "No! Chip's got enough trouble!"

CHAPTER 16

Have a Friend, Be a Friend

JIM COLLINS missed the Monday heartbreaker. It was the first time State's number-one fan had missed a game in five years. He had talked with the chief surgeon that morning at University Medical Center. Cindy was out of danger. There would be no need for skin grafts. She was receiving the best of care, and in two weeks, perhaps she would be home again. But the memory of that sudden flash and Cindy's agonizing scream still left him feeling sick. Nothing like this had happened in his life since Cindy's mom had taken ill and died, all within one tragic week.

The grief of that Sunday night had almost driven the slow, endless worry about the farm out of Jim's mind. Absentmindedly, he picked up the Tuesday morning paper and turned to the sports page to see what his boys had been doing. The bold print at the top of the column told the story.

HAVE A FRIEND, BE A FRIEND

FENCE BUSTERS LOSE AGAIN
Ramsey College Surprises Freshman Stars 6-5

"Oh, no!" Collins muttered. "Not again!" He scanned the box score, noting the absence of Byrnes, Nickels, Emery, and Burke from the lineup. "Now what?" he said aloud. "Guess Rockwell's going to let them sit it out a little while. Anyway, Gillen got a chance."

Collins sat on the front porch in his rocking chair a long time that morning. The chair had been his father's favorite for many years, and it brought back poignant memories—especially this morning. Later, when he started for University, his heart was filled with sadness. After visiting Cindy at the hospital, he delayed the disagreeable task ahead of him as long as possible. He spent an unsatisfying fifteen minutes there with the new bank president, and as he came down the broad steps, Collins ran right into Fireball Finley. The big man's attitude toward Fireball had changed immensely since the athlete had proved to be a baseball player and especially after the events of Sunday night, but he had to force a smile.

"Hello, Fred. Too bad about the game. Can't win them all though."

"We should have won that one. We couldn't do anything right. At least I couldn't. I couldn't seem to get Cindy—"

Collins nodded his head understandingly. "Lots of people have days like that, Fireball," he said softly.

"Yes, but I was awful. I just seemed sort of numb."

"Guess you weren't the only one, Fred. I read that Rockwell used Gillen. Probably didn't have a chance to use any of the others."

"They didn't show up for practice. I think they've quit for good."

"I don't understand that," Collins said slowly. "They told me they were going to let bygones be bygones. Guess I'll pay Coach Rockwell a little visit. See you later, Fred."

Collins was up to his neck in financial trouble, but his interest in State's fabulous freshmen overshadowed everything else. He headed straight for the nearest phone and asked Rock to meet him for lunch. When they met at the restaurant, Collins launched right into the subject nearest his heart.

"Tough luck yesterday, Rock. Say, what happened to the Byrnes crowd?"

Rockwell smiled wryly. "Too many headlines maybe, Jim. Some kids just can't take publicity."

"I don't believe that's it, Rock. You know, I talked to those kids last Thursday night—right after they walked off the field—and honest, Rock, they were all set to report back on Friday."

"Wonder what happened?"

"Do you think Gil Mack's story might have—"

"I don't know whether it kept them from reporting," Rockwell interrupted, "but I do know it was uncalled for. I talked to Mack about it."

"You mind if I see those kids again?"

"Of course not. You know, Jim, I've worked with kids all my life, and I've had only a handful who didn't come around one way or another. I hate to see a kid sour like this Byrnes boy. He's all right deep down inside—most kids are—but I can't seem to get through that thick head of his. I hope you can. He's worth saving."

Collins agreed with the coach. But his chief concern was the great team he had rooted so strongly for early in the season. He reasoned it was a shame to let a great team fall apart just because a kid had the wrong view on things.

That evening, after he finished his work on the farm, Jim Collins went to visit his daughter. She kissed her dad when he leaned over her bed. Never had she seen her father look so troubled, or so old.

"What's wrong, Daddy?" she asked softly. "You aren't worried about me, are you? The doctor says everything will be OK."

Jim nodded his head and smiled gently. "That's great, honey! But those freshmen of mine have got me worried."

"Now, Dad, you aren't being honest with me."

"I met Fireball this morning outside the bank. Finley didn't look very happy," Jim said.

"It isn't baseball that's worrying Fred. And I don't think it's me," Cindy said. "I think he may be worrying over the same thing that you are, Dad. Please tell me."

When Jim Collins left University Medical Center that night, he felt better than he had in months. He had told his daughter about the financial trouble that had been hanging over the farm for long, long months. And all the way out to the lonely farmhouse he could hear Cindy's words:

"Don't you worry, Dad. Nothing but good is going to happen to us now!"

Later, while Fireball and Cindy were talking on the phone, Jim Collins was meeting with Lefty Byrnes and his friends at Peppi's. Jim was having just about as much luck with them as he had had at the bank. The only member of the group he could shake was Darrin Nickels. The big catcher listened carefully and made his decision.

"I think you're right, Mr. Collins," Darrin said sincerely. "I've acted like a spoiled brat. I'll be out there tomorrow."

Darrin was as good as his word. He reported Wednesday afternoon, prepared to take any penalty from the coach. Rockwell never blinked an eye; he merely nodded and let it go at that.

Darrin Nickels couldn't be blamed for the events of that afternoon, but something put a jinx on the Fence Busters. Terrell "Flash" Sparks slipped going down the dugout steps, badly twisting his right ankle, and Diz Dean complained of a sore arm.

Grant State came in for the Friday afternoon game, and the jinx persisted. Chip played like a pro, but Fireball, Soapy, Biggie, and his other teammates performed like sandlot scrubs. Rockwell used Nickels as a pinch hitter for Soapy in the seventh, but the layoff had hurt the big receiver, and he struck out both times he came to bat. Grant walked over State by a score of 9-3.

Chip knew there was something seriously wrong with his friends. Biggie might have an off-day with the bat, but he'd never falter in his fielding and throwing. "No," Chip mused, "there's something bothering the whole bunch. They just couldn't all go bad at the same time. Soapy knows too! Well, he'll tell me tonight or else!"

It wasn't easy. Soapy tried his best to cover up, but Chip gave him no rest. "Come on, Soapy," Chip urged. "I've got to know. There's too much at stake!"

"But, Chip it . . . it's just a few bad games. We'll shake it off."

"There's more, I know it. Anything that upsets you, Biggie, Speed, and Red concerns me. That goes for Fireball too!"

"Well, if you've gotta know, it's got something to do with Jim Collins!"

"Collins? You mean—"

"That's right! You know how all the guys feel about Mr. Collins. Well, he's got money trouble."

"What's that got to do with the team playing baseball?"

"Plenty! Fireball's all upset, and he's got the rest of the guys feeling the same. I'm worried too! I like Jim Collins as much as any man I ever knew."

Chip was puzzled. It didn't make sense. "Soapy," he said impatiently, "stop beating around the bush and tell me what's going on."

Soapy took a deep breath and plunged in. "Well, he's gonna lose the farm!"

"No! How?"

"Mortgage. The bank's going to foreclose if he doesn't pay what he owes them."

"What's that got to do with playing ball?"

"But, Chip, don't you see? The bank, or at least the new president of the bank, says Collins pays more attention to baseball than he does to his farm. And, well, Fireball and Biggie and the rest of us feel like we ought to do something about it."

"Why?"

"Because he's been so nice to us, I guess. And because, because of Cindy."

That was too much for Chip. He couldn't figure it out. Sure, he liked Mr. Collins a lot. And he could appreciate how the guys felt about the farm. But what did all that have to do with State freshman baseball? And what about Cindy? This didn't make sense.

Then Soapy started to talk. He told his roommate about the tragic events that night at the Collins farm when the birthday party had come to such an unhappy end. He told Chip how Cindy had been taken to the hospital with second-degree burns and how each of the boys who had been at the party that evening was feeling personally responsible for what had happened to Cindy. The shock of it all had seriously affected their play.

"But, Soapy," cried Chip, "the Collinses are also my friends. I'm concerned about their trouble too! Here we've been friends for years, and you leave me out. I don't get it!"

Soapy was deeply sorry. "Honest, Chip, I would've told you, but Fireball and Biggie said you'd had enough trouble, and, well, you sure have. Chip, you know I tell you everything."

"Forget it, Soapy. Tell me the rest of it."

Soapy brightened. "Well, Chip, it seems that the old president of the bank played ball with Mr. Collins in the old days, and he never worried much about the farm payments. Then he died, and the new president started throwing his weight around and cracked down on past-due interest payments. They think he's trying to make a name for himself in the financial circles of the state.

"It seems Mr. Collins is way behind in payments and he can't raise the money. Fireball said he met him outside the bank yesterday morning, and Collins was as white as a sheet. And this afternoon, just before the game, Cindy told Fireball that the bank is going to foreclose in ten days. Chip, you think we can do something?"

Chip shrugged. "I don't know what, Soapy. We haven't got any money. The only person with money I know is— Hey!"

Soapy's face lit up. "You've got an idea, Chip?"

"Maybe. Let me think about it."

Chip thought about it all evening and that night too. He liked Jim Collins and he liked Cindy. It was difficult to reconcile his liking for them with burdening his boss with a problem that was little or none of his concern. He mused aloud and shook his head. "That would be an imposition."

Imposition or not, Chip made up his mind to talk to George Grayson. Jim Collins had been his friend and the friend of everyone else it seemed. Chip guessed there must be a good reason behind the old saying: To have a friend, you have to be a friend.

But Chip's resolution faltered when he reported for work the next morning. George Grayson passed the storeroom and poked his head through the doorway with a cheery good morning. Chip didn't make a move. But when Fireball clocked in a little later with a long face, Chip headed for the cashier's desk.

"You suppose Mr. Grayson would spare me a few minutes, Mitzi?"

"He's pretty busy, Chip. But for you, of course! Go on up!"

Chip was not afraid of anyone, but he would have preferred to take all his final exams in one day than to walk up the steps to George Grayson's office. But, as usual, his boss was friendly. George Grayson realized that a business owner made the most headway when his employees were happy in their work. He greeted Chip warmly.

"What's on your mind, Chip?"

"Something I just have to talk to someone about, Mr. Grayson. Do you have a few minutes?"

"Sure. What is it? The team?"

"Well, I guess it's a combination of the team and Mr. Collins. You see, the team hasn't been doing very well, and I think a lot of it is because of Mr. Collins."

Grayson took off his glasses, concern written on his face. "Jim? Can't understand that—"

"I don't mean it's his fault. It . . . it just concerns him."

"I've known Jim Collins a long time, Chip. We were classmates in high school. He was a fine ballplayer and he's been a very positive influence for the kids in this town. I think a lot of Jim, Chip. Now what about him?"

That made it easy. Grayson's receptive manner and friendly attitude were all Chip needed. He spilled the story easily and without hesitation. Grayson listened attentively until Chip finished.

"Jim Collins is a good man, Chip," Grayson said reflectively. He smiled. "No pun, now, but he deserves a lot of credit for what he's done for the kids. I guess he's done as much for the athletes at State as the Athletic Department. He's proud, too, Chip. Jim wouldn't ask anyone for help." His eyes twinkled, and a friendly smile played across his lips. "Now, Chipper, what was the real reason you came to see me about Jim Collins? Cindy Collins?"

Chip was embarrassed. "No, Mr. Grayson. I hardly know her. Honest! She and Fireball are really serious. And she's in the hospital!"

Grayson knew exactly how Chip felt about girls, and he enjoyed Chip's confusion. If Mitzi Savrill couldn't charm this young man, no one could. And Grayson knew more about the Collins matter than Chip would ever know. But he said nothing more. He gave Chip the assurance he would try to do something, but he made no promises.

During a break, Chip went over to the hospital to see Cindy. He felt he had done all he could and wished it would help the Collinses and the team, especially that afternoon at the Midland game.

Finley was no ball of fire, and Biggie and Soapy should have spent the afternoon in the library. Chip played brilliantly. He was errorless in the field and perfect at bat, going four for four. And he hustled and drove his teammates with enthusiasm. But it wasn't enough. Midland romped away with an easy 9-3 victory, and the chances of State being represented in the Little Four championship grew dimmer and dimmer.

HAVE A FRIEND, BE A FRIEND

Chip's heart was heavy, but he got a lift out of the knowledge that George Grayson knew about the problem. Anyway, it gave him something to hope for. Good news might come after the Monday board meeting at the bank. That decision might be all that was needed to help the Collinses and get the Fence Busters back on their game. When he read the paper the next morning, he knew for sure the news had better be good.

MIDLAND ROMPS OVER STATE
Easy 9-3 Victory for Visitors

Fence Busters Need Pitchers
Coach Henry Rockwell Plans Shake-Up

by Bill Bell

The fences at Alumni Field suffered little yesterday afternoon when Midland scored an easy victory over Coach Henry Rockwell's frozen freshman baseball team. It was a fast, easy game for Midland Junior College. The visitors surprised the Statesmen with a slim, 130-pound pitcher who stilled all the locals' bats with the exception of Chip Hilton's. Silent Joe Maxim, Rockwell's only remaining pitcher, was tired. Maxim has now worked two games in three days. Chip Hilton had a perfect day in the field and at bat, but the only other local who could register safely was Ozzie Crowell. Ozzie walked twice and hit twice and that was it: six hits and three runs, all unearned.

After the dull performance, Coach Rockwell stated there would be another shake-up in an effort to get the faltering Fence Busters back in the winning habit. He'll be experimenting with several players in the hopes of finding someone who can help the pitching problem.

The famed freshmen started out in grand fashion, and everyone would like to see the same group of kids tabbed the Fence Busters back in action again. That group could hit as well as any ball club that ever dashed out on a State diamond. With the Little Four championship series only a few weeks away and with the Fence Busters slipping badly, something should be done to restore the original lineup.

Lefty Byrnes, Ellis Burke, and Bob Emery liked the article. Strangely enough, they liked Bill Bell. For the first time, the trio agreed this writer knew his baseball.

"They need us," Byrnes gloated. "It takes a smart sportswriter like Bell to figure out what's wrong. Wonder what Rockwell will think now. It's about time someone told him the score. He'd never figure it out himself!"

CHAPTER 17

The Comeback Kids

GEORGE GRAYSON took a prominent role in University's civic affairs. He felt a responsibility to the community, and although he was actively involved, Grayson preferred to remain in the background. He was like that at the bank. Although one of the strongest members on the board and usually going along with the majority, Grayson seldom interjected himself into an argument.

Thomas Hemming, the former president of the bank, had given Grayson his start. Hemming had guided him through his early days as a businessman and been proud of his protégé's progress. After Hemming's death, the members of the board had selected Charles Stimley, the assistant manager, as the new president.

Stimley had long aspired to the position and started right out to prove that the methods formerly employed were outmoded. He meant to set the bank right. He bustled into the room with a sheaf of papers in his hand and called the meeting to order with a domineering formality that seemed strangely out of place after the easygoing manner of his predecessor.

"Ladies and gentlemen," Stimley began briskly, "we have a full agenda this morning, so I would like to get right down to business. I have spent the past week checking through some of our long-past-due, perhaps I should say latent, mortgages, and I am shocked at the state of the accounts. I should like to have the board's authorization to straighten them out and foreclose where necessary. Will someone put this authorization in the form of a motion?"

"I so move," Judy King said shortly.

"May I have a second to the motion?"

"Excuse me, everyone," Grayson interrupted. "Isn't it the purpose of these meetings to discuss particular mortgages and loans? I would like to know, for example, which mortgages are to be foreclosed."

A shocked silence followed. None of his colleagues had ever heard George Grayson express himself so strongly, and the interruption completely upset Charlie Stimley.

Judy King was the first to recover. "That seems logical to me," she said. "I withdraw the motion."

"Well, that's all right," Stimley said nervously. "But there's a lot of them, and there's quite a bit of business on this agenda."

"I'm not too busy to spare the time," Grayson countered.

Grayson got support from the other members of the board on that point, and Stimley began to discuss the individual cases. The Collins account was the second on the list. It was most apparent from the tone of his voice that Charlie Stimley had fully made up his mind to foreclose on the Collins mortgage.

"The Collins note shows a balance of fifteen thousand dollars with unpaid installments of some four thousand dollars and accumulated interest amounting to twenty-four hundred dollars. I've talked with Collins, and he says he is unable to meet the past-due payments and will find it difficult to meet the present year's interest payments. I gave him until today at noon to raise the past-due amounts or face foreclosure proceedings."

"What about the potential of the farm?" Grayson asked.

"What do you mean?"

"I mean, is the farm capable of supporting the mortgage? Or of supporting an increase?"

"Increase?" Stimley echoed. "With that baseball-crazy man in charge of the farm, the mortgage isn't worth the paper it's written on. He hasn't made a payment in months. And he has made no effort to make a payment on the outstanding amount for months either."

"I know the farm well," Grayson said evenly, eyeing his fellow board members. "It's a good farm, and Jim is a good farmer. He's had a few setbacks, but he's all right. Every farmer and most businesses around University have had it tough at times. That drought two years ago hit him at the worst possible time.

"His timber alone is worth ten or fifteen thousand dollars. He's got some wonderful walnut trees that are going to be worth a lot of money someday. The pines are also an asset. I'm in favor of incorporating the unpaid interest into a new note and extending the mortgage."

"How in the name of good business can you justify such a procedure?" Stimley demanded.

"Partly on the value of the farm," Grayson said softly, "but chiefly on the value of the man."

"Value of the man?" Stimley said incredulously. "That . . . that foul ball?"

"That's right, Mr. Stimley. That 'foul ball,' as you call him, has done more to set the kids of this town right than anyone I know. Men like Jim Collins are priceless to this or any community. I'm quite sure there's nothing wrong with his finances that a little time will not straighten out. I recommend we issue a new mortgage."

Judy King, Bill Hopkins, Sara Snyder, and T. C. Train couldn't figure this thing out. George Grayson always went along with the president or a consensus. There was something going on here that they didn't understand. What was it all about?

Stimley made a mistake then by interpreting their silence as disapproval for the Grayson proposal. He decided to take a definite stand. "There will be no new mortgage, Mr. Grayson," he said firmly. "As the president of this bank, I cannot jeopardize the money entrusted to my care."

"I see," Grayson said gently. He rose slowly to his feet, smiling slightly as he spoke. "Under the circumstances, I believe the only course left to me is to resign as a director of this bank."

In the stunned silence, Grayson turned to face his fellow directors. "It has always been my belief that this bank stood as an organization dedicated to the service of the community in good times and bad. An organization ready and anxious to serve its citizens—not as a profit-making institution that measures its progress by the exploitation of properties it might be able to seize through the misfortunes of the residents of the community, but—"

Sara Snyder leaped to her feet. "George," she protested, "this is ridiculous."

"That's right," Hopkins reiterated. "Downright silly. Of course, we're the friends of the citizens of the community. You—"

"Excuse me," Train interrupted. "May I interject a word? Wait, George. Tom Hemming and I founded this bank forty-three years ago. Tom dedicated his life to this bank and this community. I guess I know what he stood for better than any other person. George Grayson is right! Tom Hemming always stood by his customers in times of need. He built this bank on the cornerstone of friendship. It shall not change!"

Only the people in that room knew what transpired after Train's declaration. T. C. asked George Grayson to reconsider resigning, and Jim Collins got the surprise of his life half an hour later when he walked into the bank president's office and was received with smiling graciousness.

For one heart-rending second Collins believed Charles Stimley was being nice only because he was about to deliver bad news and didn't want a scene in the bank. But he was wrong.

"Glad to see you, Jim," Stimley said, rising from his desk and extending his hand. "I've got good news for you. The bank has decided to issue a new mortgage incorporating the back interest in a new note and making the payments a little easier."

"What? You're kidding! What a relief! Thanks, Mr. Stimley!"

"Don't thank me, Jim. Confidentially, you might buy George Grayson dinner at his favorite restaurant the next time you see him, but keep me out of it."

"You don't say! I don't get it!"

"Is it necessary?"

Collins was thinking it was, but he decided it could wait. Right now, he wanted to see Cindy. He'd go to see George Grayson afterward.

Cindy was waiting for her father with an anxious heart. She tried to cover her feelings, to act carefree and vivacious, but she wasn't fooling Fireball, who was sitting in a chair staring out the window. Finley tried to play the game too. But he wasn't successful either.

"Well, kids, guess what?" shouted Jim as he entered the room. He chuckled when he saw the anxious look in Cindy's eyes. A moment later he was telling them the wonderful news.

"Didn't I tell you, Dad, that things would be better, that we were out of the woods?" Cindy reminded him happily.

"It's our woods that the bank's giving me a new mortgage on!" Jim shouted. "From this day on, I'm working to make that farm of ours pay for itself," Jim Collins promised solemnly.

"Dad, wait. Fireball and I were thinking. We thought, maybe with our help, you could put all those baseball files into some kind of report and make it available to university and pro scouts. At least it would put all that yearly baseball clutter in your office to good use." Cindy said, smiling.

"That has some possibilities. Think the bank will give me a loan to get started?" he laughed. "What made you think of this?" Jim asked.

Fireball jumped in, "Everybody collects and trades baseball cards, Mr. Collins. I read that a college student in Ohio took his hobby and turned it into a full-time business. The Beckett Company, owned by Dr. Jim Beckett and now in Dallas, resulted from his hobby with cards and his major in math. Now he publishes sports magazines, and his price guides are considered the sports standard for collectors.

"You should see their issue on Mickey Mantle and Roger Maris. Anyway, we figured you could do something with your love of baseball and all those stats and anecdotes you collect from around the state."

"I think you've got a great idea, and I'd like to do it. But let's get Cindy out of this place, the Fence Busters winning, and the farm off to a good start first," Jim declared.

Chip Hilton was in the storeroom at Grayson's. Good news traveled fast, and it had already reached him at work. Maybe the Fence Busters would wake up now—now that there wouldn't be any more distractions to jinx the team. Chip felt the elbow of his right arm. It felt good. Dr. Terring said he could start throwing with his right arm anytime now. He wasn't ready for any heavy-duty pitching assignments, but it wouldn't be long now. Maybe he ought to try a few windups.

And that's what he was doing when Jim Collins cautiously opened the door and started the baseball jargon he was known and loved for. "Hi ya, Chip. Loosening up the old wing? How soon's that old soup bone going to be ready? Can't be very long, now, I hope."

"Feels good, Mr. Collins. Dr. Terring said I could start pitching again in about a week."

"That's great, Chip. Say—" Collins's smile faded. "Chip, I want to thank you for . . . well, for what you did. It gave me a new lease on life. Honest."

"Wait a minute, Mr. Collins. I don't know what you're talking about. You're all mixed up."

"That's what George told me you'd say, Chip. Let's leave it that way. One thing is sure. I'm not mixed up now. I guess I was, until today. Anyway, I guess words can't speak for a man's heart. Good luck, champ."

Chip thought it over. Collins knew he had talked to Mr. Grayson. So? He hadn't done anything.

Collins didn't stop with Chip. He had to tell his other kids and headed straight for Wilson Hall. They weren't there, but he soon found Byrnes, Burke, and Emery at a corner table in the student union cafeteria. It didn't take him long to tell the good news.

"That's great, Mr. Collins," Byrnes exulted.

"Well, we could make it really great news and make everyone happy if you guys would report for baseball tomorrow," Collins countered. "Guess you saw what Bill Bell wrote. Coach Rockwell would be thrilled to have you back."

"What makes you say that?"

"Because I asked him. Look, kids, everyone in town knows you three are the difference between a spot in the Little Four series and just another season. C'mon, what do you say?"

"I'll never play for Rockwell," Byrnes said decisively. "Rockwell and Hilton dug the hole they're in. Let them dig their way out of it."

"You've got Chip all wrong, Lefty," Collins said earnestly. "He's a good kid. Let me tell you something else. If it hadn't been for him, I'd never have gotten this break at the bank."

"Hilton! What did he have to do with it?"

"Everything!"

Byrnes snorted. "Hah! Guess he told you that!"

Collins smiled in resignation. "I guess it's no use. No, Lefty, Chip never said a word before or after. In fact, he pretended he knew nothing about it."

"What makes you think he did?"

"Because the only man in University who could have gotten me the break told me straight out that he did it only because of Chip."

Byrnes shook his head in disgust. "I don't get it," he said, shrugging his shoulders. "Where does he get all this credibility?"

"I don't know where he gets it. But it's my belief that he works for it. Come on, Lefty. It won't hurt. Give it another try."

Byrnes shook his head stubbornly. "Nothing doing! I wouldn't pitch for Rockwell if it meant the World Series. No, sir! Count me out! Period!"

"Well," Collins said wryly, "you three are going to cost the team the championship. They just haven't got enough power without you. What's more important right now, Rockwell's only got two pitchers left: Maxim and Dean. And they're both dead tired."

"Why doesn't he use Darrin and Murph?" Emery demanded.

"He is using them, but right now he needs pitchers."

"Oh, sure," Byrnes said bitterly. "I'd go out there, and he'd let me sit the bench just like Darrin and Murph."

"No," Collins said defensively, "I don't think Rock would let anyone sit the bench if it meant a victory. I sure wish you'd change your mind."

"No way," Byrnes said shortly. "Not me!"

"Well," Collins said forlornly, "I guess there's nothing more I can do. Seems like I can never help."

Jim Collins wasn't quite right about the last part of his unfinished observation. He had already performed his good deed. The news he had personally received that day was just what the Fence Busters needed. And starting the following afternoon, they began to prove that even the experts can be wrong about a ball club.

Waynesburg Community College caught the full onslaught. Biggie, Soapy, Fireball, and Chip climbed all over three of the Wildcats pitchers, giving Silent Joe Maxim an easy 15-3 win. The game was called after seven innings due to the twelve-run rule. Maxim just reared back, kicked, and threw the ball. His support did the rest. And it worked!

That was only the start. The team made Gil Mack, Bill Bell, and Jim Collins forget Byrnes and his two hard-hitting pals by thumping the daylights out of Oxford Community College, giving Diz Dean an 11-0 whitewash victory. Dean followed Maxim's method and again it worked.

And the Statesmen kept it up! They took to the road Friday and Saturday with Maxim beating Waynesburg Friday afternoon in a make-up for an earlier game that had been rained out and Dean taking the first game of a doubleheader from Oxford Community College on Saturday morning.

Rockwell pulled a big surprise by sending Soapy Smith to the hill in the afternoon, and the redhead came through like a twenty-game winner. So when they started back for University Saturday night, the Fence Busters were back in the running for a spot in the championship series.

University fans had watched their comeback with real appreciation, but there were a few people in town who were not particularly enthused. Lefty Byrnes was one. Lefty was having a hard time figuring it out. Like a lot of others, Lefty was puzzled by the turnaround of the Fence Busters. And he had plenty of time to think while making his deliveries each night.

It was a busy Saturday night, and Lefty had a delivery for Mrs. Grayson in the college section of University. After he rang the doorbell, Mrs. Grayson asked him to come into the foyer and called to her two grandchildren, "Kids, the pizza's here." She turned to Lefty and smiled. "Give me just a second while I get some money."

Two men were sitting in the living room just to the right of the large marbled foyer. Although he disliked the usual wait at each house, Lefty listened idly to the remarks of the two men. But his ears pricked up when George Grayson mentioned the Fence Busters.

"It looks as if the freshman ball club is back in stride. Glad to see it."

"Doesn't Chip Hilton work for you?"

"Been with me since last fall. So have Smith and Finley. Good kids too."

"I got a kick out of you setting Charlie Stimley down last Monday. Charlie's been moving a little too fast."

Grayson grunted. "Oh, I guess he's all right. Just trying to do a good job. By the way, John, I wouldn't even have known about Collins's predicament if Hilton hadn't brought it to my attention. He's a loyal kid, and he's done a lot of good things around this town. Modest too. He won't take any credit."

"I've seen him around the store. Seems to keep busy."

"He's a hustler. A real ballplayer too. Let me give you some idea of his way of thinking. I talked to him tonight when he got back on the job after the big win this afternoon at Oxford. Well, he didn't even want to talk about the game. He was looking ahead to the Carleton series. He was talking about a pitcher by the name of Byrnes."

Lefty involuntarily glanced in the hallway mirror. This was too much. Hilton again!

Grayson continued after a brief pause. "Chip said the team would breeze through if this pitcher would only play. Seems to have the idea it's his fault that this other pitcher quit the team. Some sort of a misunderstanding, I guess. Too bad!"

"Seems as if there would be plenty of room for both of them," Grayson's companion observed. "It's hard to understand why players can't get that through their heads. Especially when they're both good."

CHAPTER 18

Beanball Victory

CHIP HILTON reared back, kicked, and poured a fast-ball straight into the center of the strike zone. Mike Terring grimaced slightly as the speeding ball buried itself in his glove, but he grinned when he called for the same pitch. "That's the way, Chip! Give me the same thing now. Same spot!"

Fifteen minutes later, Terring, standing in his back-yard, called it a day. "Nice throwing, kiddo. That arm is coming along fast."

"How fast?" Chip queried.

"Well, I'd say fast enough, considering everything," Terring said slowly.

"You think I'll be ready by Saturday?" Chip persisted.

"Ready for what? Now, Chip, I just can't look at your arm and say you're ready. Your puffing up the hand of an old baseball wannabe like me isn't the best gauge to use."

"But I've been throwing hard for over a week now, and my arm never felt better."

"Playing catch isn't the same as pitching a game, Chip."

"No, but I've been throwing curves, sliders, and fastballs. Doc, my arm feels ready. I can put everything I've got into my knuckler, and it doesn't hurt a bit." Chip continued earnestly, "Rock hasn't got a single pitcher left, and we've got to play Carleton two games, Friday and Saturday. Maybe a third on Monday if we split the first two."

Terring nodded grimly, "You're telling me! Think he can use me? Haven't you ever noticed that the Rock is my friend? I guess he tells me more about his troubles than Mrs. Rockwell. I know the situation, all right."

"But if I'm OK, Doc. If my arm is well, why can't I pitch?"

"Because we haven't worked enough for one thing. Further, you couldn't pitch both games even if you *were* right. I think you might be able to pitch one of the weekend games or part of a game, but right now I'm not sure. You come here every day, play catch with your doctor, and then we'll see. But I don't want you to say a word to the coach or anyone else. Understand? If Hank starts counting on you and then it's no go, it will just about break his heart. Right?"

Chip nodded glumly and started back to Jeff. On the way, he was doing some real thinking. Maxim, Dean, and Sparks were probably out for the season. Soapy could throw the ball over the plate, but he was no pitcher. He wasn't equipped to cope with a tough team like Carleton.

"That leaves me," Chip murmured, "and I'm an uncertainty. Dr. Terring didn't seem too optimistic. I'm ready though. I know it!"

Just before he reached the dorm, Chip got an idea. He stopped and thought about it a few seconds. Then he made a decision, pivoted, and headed in the other direction.

FENCE BUSTERS

At the same moment, Lefty Byrnes was reading Bill Bell's column, and there was a sour expression on his face.

STATE FRESHMEN TAKE DOUBLE BILL
AT OXFORD
Defeat North 11-0, 14-0

Rockwell's Fab Freshmen, rapidly supplanting Gil Mack's Fence Busters in local fan acclaim, came through with a surprising double win over Oxford yesterday morning and afternoon to run their sudden and surprising victory streak to five games in a row.

This unbelievable feat was carved out by a bunch of hustlers who had to depend on two tired pitchers and a converted catcher for mound duty as well as a makeshift lineup which included players with glass arms, injured arms, football knees, and paper ankles. But it's an ill wind that doesn't blow some good.

Congratulations to Coach Henry Rockwell for a job well done. All this in the face of the crucial two-game (possibly three) series with powerful Carleton, who will be here next Friday and Saturday to play for the sole remaining spot in the Little Four championship.

So win, lose, or draw, Rock, this corner's baseball cap is off to you and your Fab Freshmen. And as a friend of yours once said to me, "The Rock? Look, Bill Bell, he can take it!" And I think you can. Frankly, I wouldn't be surprised if you took Carleton and came out on top in the Little Four series. Good luck, Coach. Keep 'em hustling.

Byrnes crumpled the paper into a ball and threw it angrily into a corner. "They're just lucky," he muttered, "Just plain fool's luck!"

He was still sitting there, thinking about the Fence Busters and his trouble with Rockwell and Chip, when someone called up from the hall downstairs to tell him some guy named Chip Hilton was there and would like to see him.

Byrnes was surprised and puzzled. "Hilton!" he managed. "What does that guy want to see me about?" He walked slowly down the steps and braced himself for the meeting.

Chip came right to the point. "Hey, Lefty. Sorry to drop by like this, but it's important." He hesitated a second and then hurried on. "Someone had to make the first move, and, well, here I am."

"What's on your mind?" Byrnes asked abruptly.

"Well, Joe Maxim and Diz Dean both have sore arms, and we've got two games with Carleton next weekend. If we could win them, we'd be in the championship series."

"Well, good for you guys!" Byrnes said shortly. "So what?"

"Just that we need you out there to win one of those games. Some of us were talking, and we figured if you would come out and get loosened up, you could win the Friday game. We might be able to struggle through the Saturday game with Soapy or someone. Anyway, a win on Friday would guarantee us a split for the weekend, and you'd be ready again next Monday if you had to. How about it?"

Byrnes shrugged. "Why should I pitch for Rockwell?"

"It isn't for Rockwell," Chip said patiently. "It's for the team."

Byrnes had no answer for that one. He just sat there mulling it over. But he wasn't thinking about the pitching or Rockwell. He was thinking about Chip Hilton. Lefty couldn't believe his hated pitching rival would sacrifice his pride to ask for help. But he felt a glow of self-satisfaction. This was more like it. Chip Hilton had come to him. Well, it was about time someone woke up. Hitting was important, all right, but good pitching was the key to pennants in the big leagues, and it was even more important in college ball.

Lefty was thinking that Chip Hilton was smarter than he'd figured. Smarter than Rockwell, anyway. But he couldn't bring himself to believe Chip had only the success of the team in mind. *There's a catch in this somewhere,* he told himself. *And I'm going to find out what it is!*

"How do I know Rockwell will let me dress even if I do come out?" he demanded.

"Because he said he would," Chip said firmly. "Dr. Terring has been working on my arm, and he said Rockwell told him just today that your uniform is still in your locker where you put it. He'd like to have you wearing it. He said he thought we could make it through if you came back. The team would sure like to have you back too. I guess you know that."

Chip could sense Byrnes was considering the idea, but there was no assurance of consent in Lefty's face. Then Chip got some unexpected assistance. Darrin Nickels and Murph Gillen breezed through the front doors of Wilson Hall. They were certainly surprised to see Chip. But when they heard why he was there, they quickly joined forces with Chip and added their support.

"What happened when you went back, Darrin?" Byrnes demanded. "Did old Rockwell put you down in front of the whole team?"

"Of course not," Darrin said impatiently. "I already told you what happened. He didn't say a word. He acted like nothing had ever happened."

BEANBALL VICTORY

"That's right," Gillen agreed.

Byrnes eyed Chip doubtfully. "All right," he said reluctantly, "I'll be out tomorrow afternoon."

"You think you can get Emery and Burke to come out?" Chip asked.

Byrnes nodded. "Sure," he said. "They'll do anything I do. They'll be there."

The unruly pitcher went to bed that night feeling better than he had for a long time. But Byrnes was worried about the meeting with Rockwell. "I'll walk right off that field if he says anything," Byrnes told himself. "I'm not going to be pushed around by that guy anymore."

The arrival of the unpredictable pitcher with Bob Emery and Ellis Burke the following afternoon created a mild sensation. Most of the players greeted them warmly. Chip was one of these, but his Valley Falls friends were more reserved. They had no use for quitters! Period!

Byrnes tried all that week to figure out why he had reversed his stand and reported back for the team. He had been hurt and puzzled when Darrin and Murph deserted him and decided to go back to the team. Lefty couldn't understand how anyone could swallow his pride and sit the bench to watch someone with half his ability starting. It didn't add up to Lefty.

"I'd never do it," Lefty muttered time and again. "Well, they came to me! Now I'm going to show Darrin, Murph, Hilton, Rockwell, and everyone else what a *real* pitcher can do. I guess the whole bunch knows now who they had to turn to for help to pull the team out of the hole."

Lefty Byrnes was a strange mixture of good and bad. Soapy could have used him for his personality research in Dr. Edna Smith's sports psychology class. Lefty had turned down an opportunity to enter the minor-league draft after his high school graduation so he could earn a college degree.

He had known the difficulties he would encounter. There had been little money available from home to help with his college expenses, but Lefty had decided to give it a try. He had landed the delivery job, and the income from his driving and financial aid were making it possible for him to attend State. But it wasn't easy. Making deliveries six nights a week from seven o'clock till midnight kept him hustling—hustling to get enough sleep and to keep up with the books and the classes. The addition of baseball meant study was a *must* every minute of the day not spent in class.

Bill Bell and Gil Mack gave the Fence Busters plenty of space that week, and on Friday the stands were packed before five o'clock for the twilight game with Carleton. Chip was out on the field early, anxious to show Rockwell his arm was ready, hoping Dr. Terring would give the good news to the coach. But Terring didn't show up, and Chip reluctantly went out to right field to chase the hard-hit flies Jim Collins was delightedly lifting high in the air and clear to the fences.

Lefty Byrnes was warming up in front of the dugout, throwing to Darrin Nickels, while Soapy Smith forlornly played catch with Eddie Anderson out in the bullpen. Joe Maxim and Diz Dean didn't even bother to limber up. Both were bitterly nursing their sore arms in the dugout.

But when the Fence Busters ran out for their fielding just before the start of the game, Soapy Smith was behind the plate. That was hard for Darrin Nickels to take. Darrin figured he'd be the battery mate for Lefty Byrnes. But Henry Rockwell hadn't finished his reconstruction job with Darrin Nickels. It still needed a little more time. So Darrin sat in the dugout beside Bob Emery, Belter Burke, and Murph Gillen, and they watched the Fence Busters on the field. Henry Rockwell shot a quick glance in their direction when he went out to fungo to the infield, but none of the quartet saw him.

Rockwell's heart was light for the first time in weeks—not because he had his Fence Busters intact again, but because he felt that Lefty Byrnes, Darrin Nickels, Murph Gillen, Bob Emery, and Belter Burke were growing up. Rock hoped they had begun to realize that baseball was a team game—a game in which every player was entitled to a chance and it was no disgrace to sit the bench. That is, if the player could do it and cheered his teammates on the field. "Well," Rockwell reflected, "the rest is up to them. They've made a good start. I'll just do a little watching now and see how they come out."

Chip was in right field. And when Rockwell lined hits out for the throws to the plate, Chip blazed the ball back with his right arm straight and true and with a perfect one-bounce hop.

Byrnes got off to a good start by striking out the lead-off hitter and getting the next two hitters on easy infield grounders. The fans weren't too friendly when Byrnes walked out to the mound to start the game, but they gave him a good hand coming back. And as the innings slipped away and Byrnes continued to throttle Carleton, the applause grew in volume and enthusiasm each time he walked back to the dugout.

Carleton started a tall, slender southpaw on the mound. And he was lightning fast. Furthermore, he was pitching tight and brushing back every power hitter who was trying to get a toehold at the plate. So State's Fence Busters, Fireball Finley, Biggie Cohen, and Chip, couldn't dig in and couldn't lace into the ball. The game turned into a pitchers' duel.

It was a fast defensive game but far from dull. Each inning the goose eggs fell steadily in line on the scoreboard, and before the players and fans could believe it, it was the bottom of the ninth and neither team had scored.

Biggie Cohen led off and went down swinging on three blazing curveballs that darted in under his hands. Red Schwartz was on deck, but Rockwell called on Belter Burke to pinch hit. Belter was uptight and didn't have a chance. He, too, went down swinging.

That brought up Chip. The hurler was afraid of Chip and tried to keep his pitches too close. Chip dueled with him until it was a full count. The three-two pitch was a slider that ducked toward the outside corner. Chip went for it and golfed the ball over first for a clean single, and the winning run was on first base. The fans were on their feet now, pleading with Andre Durley to knock one out and break up the game.

Andre crowded the plate, hunched his five-foot six-inch frame over the plate, and challenged the pitcher to drive him back. His daring was rewarded. The big lefty worked his throws down low and close and got in a hole and then walked the husky little third baseman. Chip trotted down to second base.

Soapy had caught a beautiful game and worked Byrnes as if they had been battery mates for years. And he had hit the ball. He walked up to the plate with grim determination. The visiting coach then called time and went into a huddle with the tall southpaw and the catcher. He must have known about Rock's pitching situation and that Byrnes was the only State pitcher who was available. Anyway, he decided to give Soapy a free pass to get at Byrnes. Lefty had struck out three straight times. So they walked Soapy, and that loaded the bases and put the problem squarely up to Rockwell.

The fans immediately set up a howl. "Why didn't Rockwell use a D.H. for Byrnes anyway? Now look at the spot he's put the team in. The bases are loaded and the pitcher is up." Fans were yelling for Nickels, Gillen, Emery, or Burke. Just anyone who could hit!

"Get a hitter up there!"

"What's wrong with Nickels? He can hit!"

"How about Murph Gillen?"

"Rockwell doesn't have any pitchers to bring in if he sends in a pinch hitter for Byrnes."

"What a mess!"

Byrnes had been standing in the on-deck circle, hoping Soapy would put one out and dreading the responsibility of the situation. When he heard the crowd, he felt sure Rockwell would send in a pinch hitter. He was relieved when the coach called time and walked toward the plate umpire. Then Lefty Byrnes got a shock. Rockwell walked past the ump and stood directly in front of him. He could scarcely believe his ears.

"You can do it, Lefty," Rockwell said aggressively, patting him on the back. "Go on up there and win your own game!"

"Come on, Lefty," Chip yelled from his perch on third base. "Bring me in, buddy, bring me in!"

The crowd noise was ear-splitting now, and Byrnes was in something of a daze when he stepped into the batter's box. But he heard the yells of support from his teammates above the tumult of the crowd, and above them all he could hear Chip Hilton: "Bring me in, Lefty! Bring me in!"

Lefty Byrnes was so befuddled by all the thoughts running through his mind that he never lifted the bat from his shoulder when the pitcher whipped the first pitch across the plate. He was trying to convince himself it was all true. *Imagine this,* Lefty was thinking. *Rockwell tells me to win my own game and Chip Hilton calls me buddy.* Then it happened. Byrnes came out of his fog and leaned forward to pound his bat on the plate just as the Carleton hurler fired a sharp curve high and on the inside and straight for Lefty's head. It was a hanging curve!

Lefty saw the ball coming, but he couldn't have moved to save his life. He had gone into a freeze, and the speeding ball caught him smack in the middle of the forehead. Lefty crashed to the ground like a falling tree. The crowd roar died suddenly, and time seemed to stand still. The game was forgotten. Only the umpire noted that Chip stepped on the plate when he bent down to help Rockwell lift Byrnes and carry him to the dugout.

Only a few fans noted the tally on the scoreboard. And it wasn't until those few started to leave the stands that the crowd realized the game was over and the beanball that had stunned Lefty Byrnes had won the game for the Fence Busters.

CHAPTER 19

Yahoo!

DR. MIKE TERRING was out of the grandstand and down on the field before Rockwell and Chip and his teammates had carried Byrnes to the dugout, and almost as quickly, Byrnes was out of his stupor. He muttered something about getting a hit and struggled to get to his feet. Terring held him gently on the ground while he made a swift examination. When he finished, he looked up at Rockwell, relief showing on his face, and his mouth twisted in a thankful smile.

"It isn't bad, Hank. Might have a slight concussion, but nothing serious. We'll take him to the med center for the night just to be sure. The ambulance is ready."

"How about an X-ray?" Rockwell queried.

"I don't need an X-ray," Byrnes protested, struggling once more to get up. "I'm all right! What happened?"

"You forgot to duck," Terring said gently.

"You mean I was beaned?" Byrnes demanded.

"That's right," Terring said, grinning. "But you won the game! Now, no more talking. Rock, get these kids away from here and help me get this boy on the gurney. Beat it now, you guys! Lefty, just relax."

"Can't we go along, Doc?" someone asked.

Terring shook his head. "Not now! You can visit him between eight and nine o'clock tonight."

Byrnes protested that he was all right, but Terring held open the ambulance door as the folding gurney locked in place. Rockwell went along. Chip and his teammates hurried away to get dressed, scarcely realizing they had won the game.

The irrepressible Soapy knew they had gotten the jump on Carleton, but he was subdued in his celebrating. He was holding back until he found out whether Byrnes was seriously hurt. Murph Gillen, Nickels, Emery, and Burke barged into Grayson's shortly after nine o'clock, wearing broad smiles and bearing good news.

"He's OK," Gillen said happily. "No concussion, no nothing! Nothing except a headache and the stitches of the ball imprinted on his forehead!"

"That's right," Nickels added. "Terring said he could come to the game tomorrow if there were no complications."

That was enough for Soapy. He rushed into the storeroom to tell Chip. When he returned and took his place behind the counter, he was his usual self and started right in to make up for lost time.

"You see, it was like this," Soapy said loudly, waving a spoon in the air and looking around until he had everyone's attention. "I get this idea, see, so I goes to the Rockhead, that's the coach, you know, and I says 'Rock, ol' kid, if you got any ideas on winnin' this Carleton series, you better give a little thought to getting this here Lefty Byrnes back in uniform.'"

Soapy paused to make sure he had the full attention of the crowd and then continued in a confidential tone, leaning forward and speaking in a rasping whisper. "This Rock, you know, is a fair baseball coach, but he isn't built for thinkin'. I've been takin' care of his inside baseball for years; he needs me around. Well, as I was sayin', I sell him on Byrnes, and, well, I guess you saw how the strategy worked—not that I'm lookin' for any credit, of course. But wait! That isn't half of it.

"When Chip gets on, and this Carleton pitching sharpie fills the bases—'cause he's afraid to pitch to me and, secondarily, to set up a play at any base and get at Byrnes—the Rockhead is all for sendin' in a pinch hitter. But just like always, I gets another brainstorm. 'Coach,' I says, 'remember you ain't got any more pitchers and, besides, I got a hunch this Byrnes is due!' Well, you know the rest of the story, as they say, and I don't want to pat myself on the back but—"

Soapy got patted right then! Fireball bopped him with an empty carton and everyone joined in a good-natured boo, which brought Chip out of the storeroom to see what was happening. That started Soapy off again. He was still at it when they started home at eleven o'clock. Chip Hilton was happy, and that was enough for Soapy Smith.

Lefty Byrnes had a lot of visitors that night. Jim Collins was there, proud of Lefty's victory. But deep inside he was most proud because Lefty had made such a great comeback—with himself, that is.

While Soapy was still doing his standup routine, Chip got permission from George Grayson to make a short visit to the hospital. Byrnes was sitting up in bed, with a bandage around his head and feeling impatient and disgusted. But he grinned when Chip tiptoed into the room.

"I'm all right, Chip," he said quickly. "This is a lot of nonsense. I never felt better in my life!"

"I'm very glad to hear that, Lefty. If we don't win tomorrow, I guess the coach will have to use you again on Monday. You really all right? I know what it means to get—"

Chip could have cut off his tongue. But it was too late. The words had escaped. He looked wryly at Lefty, dismay filling his eyes.

Byrnes smiled understandingly. "That's all right, Chip. I had it coming. Forget it!"

There was a long silence with each boy trying to think of some way to break the sudden tension that filled the room. Byrnes was the first to speak.

"Guess that's the opening I've been waiting for, Chip," he said haltingly. "You see, I know all about brushing back a batter. Too much, maybe—" Lefty paused, thinking back into the past. Then he continued, choosing his words carefully.

"A long time ago, when I was playing sandlot baseball, there was a man there who used to talk about pitching and the big leagues. I can see now that he just talked a good game. Anyway, he told me good pitchers used the brushback all the time, and if a batter wouldn't give ground, why you just threw one at his head and drove him out of there. He said that every big-league pitcher regarded the brushback pitch as a privilege he was permitted as a pitching tool."

"He was partly right, Lefty," Chip interrupted. "A hurler wouldn't have a chance if the batter knew every pitch would be in the strike zone. I don't know any pitcher who doesn't use a curve or some sort of sidearm pitch to fool the batter. Rock himself tells us to pitch tight to the good hitters. Of course, he doesn't tell us to throw at their heads or try to hit them."

Byrnes nodded. "I know, Chip. But you see, this man I'm talking about told me you could make any batter hit the dirt by throwing the ball *behind* his head."

"He was right about that, I guess," Chip said thoughtfully. "A batter always ducks back when a ball is thrown at him. Or else he drops to the ground. I don't believe any pitcher deliberately throws at a batter's head. I guess you and I know how hard it is to find the strike zone at times. No matter how hard a guy tries, the ball gets away once in a while. No, I don't think any pitcher deliberately tries to hit a batter. It just doesn't make sense."

"That's right, Chip," Byrnes agreed soberly, lifting his hand to the bandage on his head. "But once in a while a guy who doesn't know any better makes a mistake. I don't think the Carleton pitcher tried to hit me today. That's for sure. He wouldn't risk hitting me when it meant the loss of the game. But once in a while, a pitcher makes a mistake even when it's not in a game."

There was an awkward silence, and then Byrnes continued. "You see, Chip, what I'm trying to get at is . . . well, the ball I threw at you, the one that hit you in the elbow, I tried to hit you with that ball, Chip."

Chip smiled and shook his head. "I don't believe it! You're not that kind of guy. I don't believe it. OK?"

Byrnes tried to protest, but Chip stopped him. "Listen, Lefty," Chip said earnestly, "that's all over. My arm is as good as new, or it will be in a couple of days. Let's forget all that stuff. It's not important now. The big thing is the series with Carleton and then the championship. It's a lock now that we're all back together again. Right? I'll see you tomorrow at the game."

Chip reached the door before he remembered the other reason for his visit. He reached into his pocket and drew out a ball. It was the game ball he had picked up beside the plate.

"Here, I nearly forgot. All the guys thought you might like to have this, Lefty. It's the game ball—the one that cracked you on the head."

"You mean the beanball," Lefty said, smiling. "Now we have a Rockwell and a rockhead on the team. It took a beanball to knock some sense into this head of mine. Thanks, Chip. Thanks a lot. This ball will always remind me to keep my head right."

After Chip left, Byrnes turned the ball over and over in his hands. It was covered with names, the names of the Fence Busters. All of them! And the two names Lefty looked at the longest were Chip Hilton and Henry Rockwell.

Saturday afternoon the fans stormed the stands, wondering just who Rockwell would pull out of his hat this time to send to the mound and win the all-important game. University fans were solidly behind the Fence Busters once again—solidly behind the Comeback Kids. And as they jammed into the grandstand and the bleachers, they were full of Little Four championship talk.

Lefty Byrnes was sitting in the dugout watching the Carleton hitting practice and thoroughly enjoying his newly found feeling of peace. The victory had given Lefty a tremendous lift. But there was someone else who was most responsible, and every once in a while his eyes shifted to Chip Hilton, who was leisurely playing catch with Murph Gillen in front of the bleachers.

Lefty was in the midst of a lot of pleasant thoughts when Dr. Terring sauntered up and joined Rockwell in front of the dugout. Byrnes listened to the conversation without thinking much about it at first. Then he began to strain his ears to catch every word.

Rockwell greeted Terring morosely. "Hi ya, Doc. Looks bad!"

"What looks bad?" Terring asked, grinning amiably.

Rockwell looked at him sharply. "You can see for yourself, can't you? I don't have a pitcher."

"What about Maxim or Dean?"

Rockwell snorted impatiently. "Now isn't that an intelligent question from a medical man! You know as well as I do that they're both nursing sore arms. Neither one could throw hard enough to break a pane of glass!"

"How about Smith?"

Rockwell snorted again. "You know he's not a pitcher. He wouldn't last through the first inning!"

"Well, frankly, I don't know what you're worrying about," Terring said lightly. "You've got the best pitcher in the country all ready and raring to go! I just don't know why you don't use him."

"That's not funny! You're starting to sound like Soapy Smith! Use who?"

"Chip Hilton!"

"Chip? You mean his arm's all right?"

"It's perfect. Right now, I'd say he's faster than ever."

"But he hasn't been throwing. *Really* throwing, I mean."

"And you call yourself a baseball man? Oh, yes, he has! He's been throwing real hard for two weeks!"

"Where? When?"

Terring snickered provokingly and delayed his answer; he was enjoying Rockwell's confusion to the fullest. "Behind my house, with his own personal doctor," he said gleefully. "Chip's been throwing, and I've been doing the receiving every evening for two straight weeks. But I'm not going to be able to catch the game today. My hand is too sore from his throws! He's sharp. Real sharp!"

Rockwell's jaw squared, and he threatened Terring with his fist. "Why, you—"

Terring chuckled and winked at Byrnes. "Another thing, Rock. Chip's been ready for a week. You could have used him yesterday—if you had needed him!"

Lefty Byrnes clapped Belter Burke on the back and leaped out of the dugout, bandage and all. "Yahoo!" he shouted. "Chip, did you hear that? Chip! Doc says you're OK!"

CHAPTER 20

The Team and Rock

CHIP SMOOTHED the dirt in front of the rubber and then turned to walk behind the mound. As he swung around, he carried with him the picture of his catcher—good old dependable Soapy, thumping his glove and gazing at him with all the confidence a person could ever deserve.

Soapy Smith was a smart catcher with a strong, rapid-fire arm that sent the ball zinging to any base. And he could hit! Who could ask for a better battery mate! Chip's eyes flickered around the field, checking the rest of his teammates.

Biggie Cohen stood deep behind the baseline—six feet, four inches of first-class, left-handed first baseman—a great power hitter, fast, a strong throwing arm, and 240 pounds of heart—with all of it dedicated to his friends. You couldn't do better than that even in the big leagues. . . .

Ozzie Crowell, the squat, bowlegged, broad-shouldered keystone guardian with big hands and lightning-fast legs.

FENCE BUSTERS

A chatterbox who could back up what he had to say. Just the player to make those lifesaving double plays . . .

Speed Morris, his longtime friend and master of the long throw. An expert shortstop who could go deep into the hole, make the stop, and then throw 'em out by a step. A real competitor and as flashy in the field as any coach could wish . . .

Andre Durley, the strong, square-shouldered, hot-corner fighter. Andre fired them across the diamond like a shot from a rifle. He liked it when the going was tough and always played to win . . .

Red Schwartz, hometown friend who never wavered in his loyalty on or off the field. He played with his heart every minute of every game . . .

Fireball Finley, who was strictly a fullback. Big and rough and tough enough to bend the varsity line in the middle or off tackle. And fast enough to turn any end in the country. He could hit a ball a mile or chase a hit a mile and get it . . .

Murph Gillen, big and strong and fast. Good in the field and better than good with the bat, wood or metal. Filled with love for the game. A real competitor with guts enough to sit the bench and cheer for the teammate who had beat him out of a regular job so far . . .

Out in the bullpen, Terrell "Flash" Sparks, Diz Dean, and Silent Joe Maxim—an injury-stricken crew of pitchers who never quit and who cheered for each other every time each faced a hitter . . .

In the dugout, the guys who reported every day for practice and then rode the bench during the games. Leopoulos and Anderson and Roberts and McGuire. Real competitors. They knew what sports were all about . . .

On the bench, a coach who never let his players down—a man who worked as hard as they did—a leader who played the game hard and straight and taught clean baseball . . .

Last, but not least, the four great ballplayers sitting side by side in the dugout. Great teammates once they got straightened out. Chip could hear them chattering in the dugout, cheering the players on the field. Lefty Byrnes, Bob Emery, Belter Burke, and Darrin Nickels were really part of the freshman team now . . .

A & M, Cathedral, and Tech were in for a big surprise in the Little Four championship series. Now that the Fence Busters were intact again.

"Chip! What's the matter? The umpire's irritated! He's yelled 'Play ball' three times!"

Chip hadn't heard a thing, but he reassured Soapy and told him he was ready. And even as he told his buddy everything was all right, Chip was thinking he was the luckiest guy in the world.

Carleton meant business. The leadoff man hit from the third-base side of the plate. Crowding for every inch, he was determined to start it off right. He was short, broad, and had good eyes. Chip figured this hitter would make him groove it in before he flickered an eyelash. Chip teased him with a fastball, low and outside, and the little guy never twitched a muscle. A slider inside around the belt got the same treatment. Chip hooked the two-and-no pitch around the knees, and the resounding and all too familiar crack meant the hitter had laid all the good metal on the ball. That meant distance!

Chip didn't look right away, and that's the reason he didn't see Finley take off without a backward glance and make a backhand stab at the ball. But he did look up in time to see Fireball haul it in and toss the ball to Schwartz. The crowd roar stilled the little shout he gave, but he stood there until Fireball gave him the high sign.

"Whew! That was close," Chip murmured to himself.

The second hitter rapped Chip's first pitch right back at the mound. It was a high bouncer, a sure hit through the middle if Chip hadn't leaped high in the air at precisely the right instant to spear the ball. He threw the runner out at first and breathed another sigh of relief. But he was worried. Four pitches and two hard blows that had all the earmarks of sure hits except for two lucky stabs.

Chip took a long time before he looked for Soapy's sign. It was the first time in a long while that his confidence had been shaken. Maybe the layoff had done something to his arm. What if Dr. Terring was wrong?

Soapy must have known what Chip was thinking because he called time and came striding out along the alley. "You OK, Chipper? Your arm all right?" he asked anxiously.

"Don't know, Soapy. It feels all right, but those two balls were hit hard."

"Purely coincidental," Soapy said vigorously. "They had their eyes closed. C'mon, throw it in! You've got lots of help!"

Chip threw it in, and he got the help—not only that inning but through those which followed too. And he needed all the help and all the breaks he could get because the Carleton pitcher was at his best!

Tall, wiry, and determined, this opposing pitcher had blinding speed. He was wild enough to keep the hitters off balance, but he had enough control to keep out of trouble. Not that the Fence Busters didn't get to him, but they couldn't put their hits and breaks together.

Going into the top of the fifth, Chip suddenly realized he hadn't given up a hit and was building up to the magic one. For some time, he had noted the change in the crowd, but it wasn't until he glanced out toward Fireball in center field and saw the goose eggs on the scoreboard that he realized where he was headed. He didn't feel too good about it: Carleton runners had been on base almost every inning. He would have been in trouble time after time had it not been for the miraculous fielding of his teammates.

In the bottom of the eighth, with two long rows of goose eggs decorating the scoreboard, Durley led off with Gillen on deck and Soapy in the hole. Andre hit from the third-base side of the plate and was dangerous. The third baseman stood only five-six, but he was powerful and possessed a good eye. The Carleton pitcher fenced with Durley until the count was two and two and then broke Andre's resolve on a sharp-breaking curve for the third strike.

That brought up Murph Gillen. Gillen was a left-handed power hitter. But Murph wasn't thinking about the fences. He wanted desperately to get on base for a number of reasons. He would have taken a beanball with a laugh if it meant he could reach first. He was ice up there. He waited the pitches out until the count was three and two and then blasted the ball over the second base-man's head and through right-center clear to the fence. And Murph never stopped until he was perched on third.

That solidly hit triple delighted the fans and brought the Carleton coach out to the mound. Soapy took a long time selecting a bat, his freckled face set with grim deter-mination. But when he started up to the plate, Rockwell bounded out of the dugout and called to him.

"Hold it, Soapy," Rockwell said softly, grasping the catcher by the arm. "I've got to do something important right here. Sorry, kiddo." He turned to the dugout. "Nickels!" he called sharply. "Hit for Smith!"

Darrin nearly jumped out of his skin; he moved like a streak getting to the bat rack. He was afraid Rockwell would change his mind. Darrin had been doing a lot of thinking in the dugout. The big receiver was no fool, and he realized there was more to this than being a pinch hitter. Smith had hit two for three and was catching a great game. Besides, Soapy had caught Chip Hilton for years and knew every move his pitcher made. As he fumbled with the bats, Darrin's thoughts nearly floored him. "Oh, what a chump I've been," he muttered. "If I can only—"

Everybody in the park was trying to figure the play. Bottom of the eighth, no score, one down, man on third. Good pitcher working, good hitter at the plate. Would Rockwell squeeze or hit? Nickels didn't look much like a push-along type. The big player weighed 230 pounds and was as tough as steel!

Jim Collins was one of those in the stands who was figuring. Beside him sat his pretty daughter Cindy. Her lovely eyes were on the outfielders—or rather, one outfielder.

Jim always thought out loud at a ball game, and today he was surrounded by a big circle of friends and fans. They were listening too. Collins had called everything right so far.

The baseball fan was emphatic. "He'll lay it down and squeeze in the run! He's got to! With Hilton pitching like there's no tomorrow, he can't afford to do anything else. One run's as good as a hundred the way Chip's going!"

The Carleton infielders closed in at baseline distance; they were poised for the play at the plate, a bunt or a hit. The pitcher kept his throws high and low, nothing good, and the count went to two and one, two balls and a called strike. Then, on the two-and-two pitch, Darrin laid it down the third-base line just as if he had been doing that all his life.

"What did I tell you!" Collins exploded. "What did I tell you!"

Cindy Collins put her left hand under Jim's arm.

The Carleton third baseman was in like a shot and set for the play at home. But he didn't have a chance. Gillen went for the plate. He drove through the Carleton receiver blocking his path as though he wasn't there and spread-eagled himself on the plate as if he meant to pin it to the clay for a three count. The Carleton third baseman cast a rueful glance at the plate and threw to first, getting Darrin by ten feet.

But it didn't matter right then, not to the fans. They were stomping and cheering, and Gillen was mobbed by his teammates all the way to the dugout. That brought Chip up, and he tried to add to the insurance. But the best he could do was a long, high fly that carried to the right-center fence. The center fielder easily pulled it in, and that was that!

The fans gathered in Alumni Field that Saturday afternoon had been pulling with all their hearts for the tall, hungry blond hurler who had experienced so many tough breaks during the season.

"The kid's been playin' with one arm all banged up!"

Chip walked out slowly for the top of the ninth with a million thoughts flooding his mind, each trying to get the most attention. Three outs! Three hitters, and the Rock would have a chance at the Little Four championship. Then Soapy, Biggie, Speed, Red, Fireball, and all the team would get the reward they deserved for fighting so hard and so doggedly through the season.

FENCE BUSTERS

Nickels's face was grim, and every return of the warm-up pitches to the mound expressed the pent-up determination he felt. The rest were all the same.

In the dugout, Lefty Byrnes was throwing every ball with Chip. The happy hurler had pulled an about-face in every way. He, Emery, and Burke pulled and swayed every time a pitch missed the strike zone. The Fence Busters were a team again, on the field and on the bench!

The tough little leadoff man who had caused so much trouble all through the game was up there again. And he got the jump on Chip. He worked the count to three and two. Nickels called for a curve, but Chip shook him off. The little guy had already tagged two of those!

Darrin then called for the slider, and Chip gave it all he had. The ball headed for the outside corner and broke across the plate right under the wrists. The Carleton batter hit it all right, but on the handle of the bat, and the ball went spinning crazily down the first-base line.

Biggie pounced on the ball like a big cat and pivoted just in time to avoid the charging runner. Without pausing, it seemed, Biggie drilled the ball like a flash of light straight into Ozzie Crowell's hungry glove. Ozzie couldn't have dropped the ball if he had tried. In fact, he put on a pantomime pretending he had to pry each of his glove fingers off the ball one at a time.

The fans ate that up. It was a partial release from the excitement that had kept mounting and mounting inside their chests and they had been trying to hold in.

The second hitter, batting from the third-base side of the plate, had hit the ball hard, twice in a row, right up the middle. Chip had fielded the first one, but the second had streaked past him on the third-base side of the rubber and was on its way until Speed Morris had come from nowhere, it seemed, to pick up the ball on a dead run behind second base. The speedster had twisted in the air and thrown a perfect strike to Cohen to nip the runner by a whisker. That brought down the house and was just a sample of the kind of support Chip had been receiving.

Chip, trying to keep the ball in close to the hitter, got behind two and no. A sharp breaking curve caught the outside corner for a called strike, and then Chip came back with the fastball. The batter met it right on the nose, and the ball didn't rise three feet above the ground. It headed straight for Andre and nearly bowled him over, but he held on to it. That made it two away.

And now, Chip and the Fence Busters were one out away from the championship series. Henry Rockwell was sitting deep in the dugout, leaning forward with his hands supporting his chin, and living through one of those priceless, high-premium moments a coach dreams about. Rock's eyes were fixed on Chip, and all his hopes were pinned on the slender youngster's arm.

The batter was the Carleton center fielder. Hitting left-handed, he had struck out twice and hit one clear to the right-center fence. Fireball had practically climbed the fence to snag that one. Chip worked the count to one and two and then tried to slip in a curve. He slipped it in all right, but the batter pivoted and met the ball with the fat part of the bat and pulled a low-rising line drive over first.

Chip had finished in his fielding position, his feet spread and arms hanging loose, and was ready for a play. And he stayed right there, turning only his head to see Biggie leap high in the air in a futile effort to reach the ball.

Murph Gillen was an even six feet in height and weighed 210 pounds. No one would ever have known it, judging by the sprinter's start he made as he drove toward the ball. Gillen had shifted a bit to his left out in right field, but he was far away from the drive. The ball was far ahead and over to his left.

Chip wanted to close his eyes, but something held them open. Just when it seemed the ball had dipped to hit the ground, he saw Gillen dive. Gillen dove for the ball and went head over heels and back up on his feet with the precious prize clutched tightly in both hands.

The first-base umpire was right on the play, and Biggie was right behind him. Then when the umpire's thumb went up over his head, Biggie grasped Gillen in his powerful arms and lifted him high in the air, shouting over and over, "What a play! What a play!"

When Biggie put Gillen down, much to Murph's delight, they were too happy to hear the booming shouts and continuous roar following the umpire's gesture. Then Gillen got quiet, and he said something that was a lot more important to Biggie than the grandstand catch.

"That one was for Chip," Gillen said grimly. "For Chip and the team and Rock—"

Gillen never finished that sentence because Biggie had him up in the air again, and then they were surrounded by Soapy, Darrin, Speed, and nearly the entire team. And when Byrnes, Emery, and Burke arrived, they grabbed Chip and up he went beside Gillen.

Chip and Murph were trying to scramble down from the shoulders of their happy teammates, but it was no use. So they substituted a "put-and-take" contest instead as each tried to force the game ball into the hands of the other.

Rockwell, Terring, and Collins came rushing up to join the celebration, and that made it complete. The Fence Busters were indeed a team again.

THE TEAM AND ROCK

. . .

When CHIP HILTON accepts a job as a member of the coaching staff at a summer sports camp, the very last thing he expects to run into is a football problem. The appearance of a sophomore receiver at State University causes Coach Curly Ralston a surprise football problem too. Your respect for a player who sacrifices personal glory for the sake of the team will grow as you read Coach Clair Bee's next story in the Chip Hilton Sports series . . . *Ten Seconds to Play!*

Afterword

I AM honored and privileged to be able to reflect upon the great Hall of Fame coach and author Clair Bee. For my generation, Coach Bee was an icon of a basketball coach whose influence on the game was immense. When I began my own career coaching college basketball at the age of twenty-five, some of the training and coaching methods of Coach Bee were at the very root of the philosophy I was trying to develop. He was extremely innovative, well organized, and recognized worldwide as one of the great teachers of the game.

Looking back, it is unfortunate that the modern communication networks we know today were not in place during his era. His influence would have been even greater. He overcame this, however, by establishing himself as a very gifted author. His first works were basketball teaching textbooks on coaching and playing methods, which many others and I still have in our libraries today.

AFTERWORD

Coach Bee soon moved beyond technical works as an author. His wonderful Chip Hilton series of books became the primary reader for a generation of sports-minded youth. While they were enjoying the games and competition that Chip Hilton was engaged in, they were also learning a great deal about integrity, sportsman-ship, teamwork, unselfishness, and responsibility. Through his Chip Hilton character and stories, Coach Bee positively influenced the youth of America in a big-ger way than any before him, or perhaps since.

As one whose entire life and career have been involved in the sport of basketball, the thing I treasure the most about Coach Bee was his respect for the game. In a present-day atmosphere where the game is so often disrespected, where there seem to be far more takers-from than givers-to our great sport, Coach Bee and his legacy of respect for and major contribution to the game are to be even more treasured.

DAVE GAVITT
Chairman, Basketball Hall of Fame

Your Score Card

I have I expect
read: to read:

____ ____ 1. **Touchdown Pass:** The first story in the series, introducing you to William "Chip" Hilton and all his friends at Valley Falls High during an exciting football season.

____ ____ 2. **Championship Ball:** With a broken ankle and an unquenchable spirit, Chip wins the state basketball championship and an even greater victory over himself.

____ ____ 3. **Strike Three!** In the hour of his team's greatest need, Chip Hilton takes to the mound and puts the Big Reds in line for all-state honors.

____ ____ 4. **Clutch Hitter!** Chip's summer job at Mansfield Steel Company gives him a chance to play baseball on the famous Steeler team where he uses his head as well as his war club.

____ ____ 5. **A Pass and a Prayer:** Chip's last football season is a real challenge as conditions for the Big Reds deteriorate. Somehow he must keep the team together for their coach.

____ ____ 6. **Hoop Crazy:** When three-point fever spreads to the Valley Falls basketball varsity, Chip Hilton has to do something, and fast!

YOUR SCORE CARD

I have   I expect
read: to read:

About the Author

COACH CLAIR BEE is considered one of the greatest basketball coaches of all time—both collegiate and professional. His winning percentage, 82.6, ranks first overall among any major college coach, past or present. His name lives on forever in numerous halls of fame. The Coach Clair Bee and Chip Hilton awards are presented annually at the Basketball Hall of Fame honoring college coaches and players for their commitment to education, personal character, and service to others on and off the court. He is the author of the twenty-four-volume bestselling Chip Hilton Sports series, which has influenced many sports and literary notables, including best-selling author John Grisham.

more great releases from the

Chip Hilton Sports Series

by Coach Clair Bee

The sports-loving boy, born out of the imagination of Clair Bee, is back! Clair Bee first began writing the Chip Hilton series in 1948. During the next twenty years, over two million copies of the series were sold. Written in the tradition of the *Hardy Boys* mysteries, each book in this 23-volume series is a positive-themed tale of human relationships, good sportsmanship, and positive influences—things especially crucial to young boys in the '90s. Through these larger-than-life fictional characters, countless young people have been exposed to stories that helped shape their lives.

WELCOME BACK, CHIP HILTON!

Vol. 1 - Touchdown Pass
0-8054-1686-2

Start collecting your complete Chip Hilton series today!

available at fine bookstores everywhere